FOREVER IN FLOWERS

JUNIPER CREEK GOLDEN YEARS

BRENNA BAILEY

BOOKMARTEN PRESS

Published by Bookmarten Press

Forever in Flowers

ISBN (eBook): 978-1-7382941-0-7
ISBN (paperback): 978-1-7382941-1-4
ISBN (large print paperback): 978-1-7382941-2-1

Cover design by Cover Ever After
Edited by Jessica Renwick

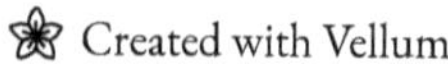 Created with Vellum

CHAPTER ONE

LORETTA

95 DAYS UNTIL THE WEDDING

*L*oretta Vogel tried to school her expression as she stared at the ugliest chandelier she'd ever seen. The gaudy gold-and-crystal monstrosity hung in front of her in the middle of Mabel's Antiques. Greg, Mabel's grandson, stood proudly before it, and her friend Evvie pressed her lips together, clearly trying to hide a grimace.

"What do you think?" He crossed his arms and raised his eyebrows as if waiting for her impressed reaction. "I'll even give you ten percent off, since you live in town."

Technically, she lived right outside of town, but that wasn't important.

Now, how could she let Greg down gently?

"Erm," Evvie said, tilting her head from side to side and toying with the end of her long white braid. Loretta had known Evvie for years, but recently, they'd become much closer; a few months ago, Evvie had started dating Loretta's older brother, Matthias. "It's certainly something, isn't it?"

Greg nodded, clearly not picking up on Evvie's tone. "You

said you were looking for a statement piece, right? This would definitely make a statement." Greg's earnestness was almost painful.

"It would," Loretta said, glancing at Evvie, who shrugged helplessly. She frowned at the chandelier. Uncomfortably bulbous pieces of gold protruded from the chandelier arms as if the creator had been aiming for an abstract art piece rather than a practical light fixture, and the crystals were distinctly phallic in shape. "I'm just not sure it's the type of statement I'm looking for."

Greg's expression fell. "Oh. Are you sure? I could give you twenty percent off instead. Call it a seniors' discount."

Was that supposed to sway her decision? Sure, she was seventy-one, but she didn't need a seniors' discount at an antique store. "No, no," Loretta said. "I'm sure. It'll be the perfect statement piece for someone else, just not for me."

She thanked him then wove through the tables of antiques to the door, trying not to knock anything over. As soon as she emerged from the shop into the fresh March air, she breathed a sigh of relief.

Evvie giggled as they walked down the sidewalk, Main Street stretching before them in either direction. Downtown Juniper Creek was quiet, typical for a Tuesday in late winter. "That chandelier was *horrendous*. Did you see the crystals?" She dropped her voice. "They looked like penises."

"They really did." The two women burst out laughing, Loretta wiping tears from her eyes. They paused to catch their breath.

"Sorry that wasn't a success," Evvie said. "And you haven't found anything elsewhere in town?"

Loretta shook her head. "I've checked all the stores on Main Street. Nothing fits." She'd been looking for the perfect light fixture for the barn since its renovation had started in January. It was almost ready to be painted now, but she still didn't have that essential *thing* that would pull everything together. Something to make it the perfect rustic wedding venue.

"Well, there's still time. Maybe Minnie or Eleanor will have an idea to help."

She and Evvie walked to her car, which was parked across the street in front of Minnie's flower shop, Emily's Garden. "Maybe."

Loretta owed Evvie for finding her first clients for her new wedding venue business: Evvie's friends, Minnie and Eleanor. Loretta knew them in passing and she'd even had coffee with them once, but she didn't know them well enough to call them friends. They'd gotten engaged on the winter solstice, and Evvie insisted they'd jumped at the chance to be the farm's inaugural wedding. The date was set for June—a tight deadline, but hosting Minnie and Eleanor's wedding would be fantastic for publicity. Since they were both well-connected florists in Juniper Creek, they'd likely invite much of the town to the event.

No matter what, Loretta would make the wedding happen. All she wanted with this venue was to make people happy. To make the barn useful again, to make *herself* useful again. To give her home and herself new life. She'd been stuck in the fog of her depression for too long, and she'd only started to break out of it when Matthias came to stay in November. This new business venture filled her with energy and a sense of renewal—not to mention trepidation—and the sooner she could get started with it, the better.

The barn had been a mess while it was under construction, but now it was fit enough for Minnie and Eleanor to view it, and Loretta had been preparing to give them a tour that afternoon.

The rest of the farm wasn't quite ready yet. There weren't any animals besides Loretta's beloved hens, which simplified things; it hadn't been anything other than a hobby farm since her father passed away thirty years ago. But she still wanted to put in a pathway to the barn, a fence to direct people away from the house, and a gazebo where guests could visit and take photos. There were other logistics to work out as well, like washrooms and space for caterers, but she had ideas for those. She just hoped Minnie and Eleanor believed in her ideas as much as Evvie and Matthias seemed to. The last thing Loretta wanted was to disappoint them today.

As the women drove out of town with Loretta at the wheel, Evvie patted her arm. "Trust me, they'll love it. They've been so excited to see what you've done with the place!"

Loretta knew Evvie meant to comfort her, but her stomach roiled. It was all too easy for people to imagine a place as one thing and far overshoot reality.

Matthias came out of the farmhouse as they pulled into the driveway. Although he'd lived at the farm since November, he spent much more time at Evvie's place these days.

He wore jeans and a black Henley, and a smile spread across his face when he saw Evvie. His gaze was fond, his expression warm, and—not for the first time—an unidentifiable feeling rose in Loretta's chest at the sight. He was seventy-four years old, three years older than her, and he had found love again. His true love, he'd said more than once. Looking at him and Evvie together, Loretta found him impossible to disbelieve, even if she was wary.

"There you are," he said, leaning toward Evvie so she could stand on her tiptoes and kiss him on the cheek, just above his trim brown beard streaked with silver. Just like Loretta, his hair was still dark, graying only around his temples. Their mother had been the same way, her hair still dark and curly on the day she passed.

Matthias slung an arm around Evvie's shoulders, his black shirt a stark contrast to Evvie's bright purple sweater. Loretta suppressed a smile even as the feeling in her chest grew and made her want to shrink into herself.

"Did you think we were going to be late?" Evvie asked.

"No." Matthias swung open the door and they walked into the house, Loretta following behind. "Etta is never late. You, on the other hand . . ."

Evvie swatted him lightly, laughing. "You love me anyway."

"I do." He grinned then turned to Loretta. "How are you feeling about today? Are you ready?"

She shrugged and slipped off her boots. "I think so."

"It will be fine," Evvie said. "This place is lovely, even unfinished. And if you introduce Eleanor to the girls, she'll love it even more."

That was promising. Anyone who loved Loretta's chickens had good taste, in her opinion. Even Matthias had developed a soft spot for them, especially Persephone for some reason.

Matthias nodded. "Minnie and Eleanor are pretty easygoing."

"I'll take your word for it."

She busied herself by boiling the kettle, setting out mugs and tea, and laying out a plate of cookies Evvie had baked the day before. Every few minutes, she glanced at the clock on the stove, watching the time tick down until her guests arrived.

Finally, a knock on the front door startled Loretta out of her nervousness. She put on her best customer service smile, ignoring her pounding heart and trying not to wring her hands. She grasped her silver Magen David necklace, taking comfort in the shape of the metal against her palm. When they celebrated Hanukkah a few months ago, she'd pulled it from the box she'd kept of her mother's things. It had become a sort of anchor for her, reminding her of who she was. She was getting sentimental in her golden years, clearly. Although, if she was honest, she'd always been sentimental.

Evvie came to stand beside her and gave her an encouraging nod, so she pulled open the door.

Through a chorus of hellos, Evvie hugged her friends while Matthias hung back in the living room. "You remember Minnie and Eleanor?" Evvie gestured to her friends.

Eleanor wore a gorgeous green dress that flowed down around her immaculate black boots, the hem embroidered with white flowers. Her salt-and-pepper hair hung in glossy waves by her shoulders. "Lovely to see you again, Loretta." Her Scottish accent was strong—she'd just moved to Juniper Creek the previous summer.

"You too."

Loretta reached out her hand, and Eleanor's palm was soft against hers.

Minnie stepped forward, brushing a white curl out of her eyes. She was dressed much more subtly than Eleanor in a dark-blue coat and gray pants. "Thank you for doing all of this for us," she said. Her grip was firmer than Eleanor's, much more businesslike.

"Of course. I just hope you like the place."

As Loretta showed them around the grounds, she couldn't help but imagine how they might see it all: old, slightly musty, muddy from the spring rain. She led them into the barn, and Eleanor moved to the middle, spinning slowly in a circle as she looked around.

"It's charming," she said, making Loretta still for a moment.

"Oh." She tried to mask her surprise as Evvie shot her a look that said *I told you so*. "It is, isn't it? And it will be even more charming once it's painted and full of light."

"What do you think, darling?" Eleanor asked Minnie.

"I can see it." Minnie moved to Eleanor's side, threading her arm through her fiancée's. The two of them were so comfortable together, Loretta could easily see why they were getting married. "I remember what my shop looked like before I transformed it into Emily's Garden. It was a mess, really. Way worse than this. The renovation was a nightmare, but I wouldn't exchange that experience for the world. This place will be just as beautiful, I'm sure." She smiled, and her hope for this venue shot straight to Loretta's heart.

"Thank you, Minnie. I really appreciate that." It made her feel like she was glowing. "Shall we go inside for tea? I can show you a few sketches of what it will look like when it's finished."

They followed her into the house, and a pressure seemed to lift off Loretta's chest. The afternoon was going well. Minnie and Eleanor seemed genuinely excited to have their wedding in the barn.

The five of them sat around the kitchen table with their

drinks. Once everyone settled, Loretta got her sketchbook and let Minnie and Eleanor flip through it. They made noises of appreciation as they went, and a wave of warmth washed over Loretta. It meant the world to her that they saw her vision and wanted to be part of it.

"This is perfect," Eleanor said, smiling and handing the sketchbook back to Loretta.

"I agree." Minnie sipped her tea. "I got a hint of this while we were in the barn, but now I really see what you mean. It's a lovely space for a wedding venue."

"Oh, fantastic!" Evvie clapped, the dimple on her left cheek shining. "I knew you two would love it. A farm seems like the perfect venue for the wedding of two florists, doesn't it?" She looked at Matthias, who nodded in agreement.

It struck Loretta that she was sitting at a table with two perfectly happy couples, one of whom was getting married, and the other who seemed so well-suited for each other, she thought they were almost *too* perfect.

Then there was Loretta. Single, living with her chickens. Not that there was anything wrong with that. But surrounding herself with people happily in love made her remember how she had felt with Gail twenty years ago. She thought Gail had been the one, that they'd be together for the rest of their lives. She had a sketchbook full of portraits of Gail, of the two of them together, of the visions Loretta had had of them with their own hobby farm.

But that hadn't been Gail's dream.

"Etta?" Matthias nudged her foot, and she realized someone had been talking to her.

"Sorry, I zoned out for a second." She sipped her tea to bring herself back to the present and burned her tongue, wincing.

"It's alright," Eleanor said. "I was asking if we could help at all with prepping the barn."

Loretta shook her head. "Oh, no, you don't need to do anything. I'll give you a discount on the booking anyway since you're our first clients. Of course, you're free to come by and see the progress whenever you like. And if you have any preferences for decor or an archway—anything specific you want us to handle —just let me know."

"Thank you again, Loretta, we really appreciate it," Minnie said.

"Of course."

"How's the rest of the planning coming?" Evvie asked the happy couple.

"We've just started, really," Eleanor replied. "Honestly, we were struggling for a bit."

Minnie tensed but relaxed again when Eleanor grasped her hand.

Eleanor continued, "We couldn't exactly agree on what we wanted, and everything we looked at didn't feel *right*. It didn't feel like us. But now we've got a better idea of what to do, and one of my friends from back home is exactly the person we need to get it done." She turned to Loretta and Matthias to explain. "Joyce is a wedding planner—well, retired, but she worked for decades in the wedding business. We met in London, but she lives in northern Scotland now with her family; they run a boat tour company up there. I reached out to ask her if she'd help us. Our wedding won't be huge—"

"Thank goodness," Minnie said.

"—so we're not worried about the timeline. And anyway, I miss seeing Joyce. I told her she could help us plan over video call, but she insisted on coming to help in person!" Eleanor beamed, then her smile faltered. "I sort of lost touch with her after Amara passed, and this is an opportunity for us to visit and become close again."

Loretta often forgot Eleanor had been previously married— her wife had passed away a decade ago from cancer.

Matthias nodded. "I get that." He had left his former band-mates in LA, and although one of them—Nick, the lead singer— had come to visit for the holidays, Matthias struggled with the separation from his friends. They were essentially his brothers.

"You talked to Joyce last night, right?" Minnie asked. "Isn't her flight soon?"

"She's flying in on Friday, yes. I hope you won't mind having someone else to liaise with," Eleanor said to Loretta.

"I don't mind." She did, actually—she wasn't much of a people person—but she knew she'd have to talk to all kinds of people if she wanted to host weddings in her barn. She rubbed her thumb on the smooth surface of her mug. "I'm sure we'll get along."

"I was thinking, actually," Eleanor said, "that Joyce could help you with your business if you want. She worked for an agency at first, but then she started her own wedding planning business and built it up successfully. I'd be happy to ask her for you."

Loretta froze. She *had* been struggling with getting the business going beyond the basics, but she didn't know if she wanted help from a complete stranger. "Um, I'll keep that in mind. Thanks, Eleanor."

Minnie smiled, her brown eyes kind. "Well, we should get going," she said, scooching her chair back. "Thank you for the tour, and for the tea and cookies."

"You have our numbers, right?" Eleanor asked, and Loretta nodded.

"I also have Evvie," she said. "I doubt she'd let me lose contact with two of her best friends."

Evvie winked at her. "You're right about that. I'm the glue that keeps us together."

Minnie snorted, and Eleanor nudged her. "We'll be in touch again soon. Why don't we meet at the diner after Joyce settles in to make our plans more official? I'm sure she'd like to hear about the venue progress, and then you can meet her."

That didn't sound like the most fun dinner, but Loretta couldn't turn down her first clients. "Sounds good to me."

She waved them off and stood in the doorway, then she blew out a breath. It was real. It was really happening. Loretta was opening her own business.

CHAPTER TWO

JOYCE

*J*oyce Grant left the lights off and tip-toed through her daughter's kitchen, feeling like a thief. Except thieves didn't usually leave a fresh-baked loaf of bread on the counter and wash the dirty mugs in the sink. She thought about wiping off the table too, but she had to draw a line somewhere.

She considered waiting for her daughter to get home so Joyce could be sure she was safe, but that would likely be too much. Instead, she retraced her steps to the back door and let herself out. She had just turned the key in the lock when someone cleared their throat behind her.

Bollocks. She knew she should have come earlier.

She whirled around. "Tori! You're home early." Her daughter's expression made her grimace.

"Mum, what are you doing?" Tori put her hands on her hips, her lips pressed together. With her blond hair up in a bun, she looked just like Joyce had thirty years ago even though they weren't biologically related. Her nametag for the wildlife tours she gave on the *Guillemot Guide* was still pinned to her jacket.

"I came by to check on things, that's all," Joyce said, trying to be the picture of innocence.

Tori shook her head. "What did you do this time?"

There was no getting out of this one. Joyce sighed and zipped up her coat so she had an excuse to avoid Tori's gaze. "I dropped off a loaf of bread, and I did a few dishes. Nothing to worry about."

"We have two loaves in the freezer already, and Burt has been asking me if we have cleaning gremlins." Tori threw her hands up. "I'm thirty-eight years old, Mum. You've got to stop doing this!"

Joyce scowled. "Since when is it a crime for a mother to take care of her daughter?"

Tori's expression softened, but she still frowned. "It's not a crime. But I can take care of myself. I love you, and I appreciate how much you've helped me, but I'm okay now." Joyce opened her mouth to object, but Tori said, "Even if I wasn't, Burt will be home soon."

As if Burt could replace Joyce.

"Well." Joyce huffed and pulled the strap of her tote bag firmly over her shoulder. "When I'm in Canada, you'll miss those loaves of bread."

That brought a smile to Tori's face—a small one, but still a smile. "You're probably right. Say hi to Da and Dad for me, yeah?" She wrapped Joyce in a hug, holding her close for a second. Every time Tori hugged her, Joyce felt smaller, as if she shrank with the passing of the years.

On her walk home, she brushed off Tori's complaints. Her daughter would cool off once Joyce left that weekend. She'd have plenty of time to do so, since Joyce would be gone for three and a half months.

Joyce hadn't been away from home for that long in . . . well, possibly ever. She could hardly fathom leaving Tori for an extended period, even if Tori was right when she said she was okay now. The boating accident had happened years ago. Tori had worked with a therapist since then to help with her PTSD, and Joyce hadn't had to accompany her on the boat for the past few months to make sure she was okay. But still, Joyce worried about her.

When Eleanor had called and asked if Joyce would plan her wedding in Juniper Creek, Joyce had hemmed and hawed about it for ages. By the time she made up her mind that she'd take the chance and go, she thought Eleanor would have given up on her. She hadn't though, and the relief that had washed through Joyce had been stronger than she'd expected.

Joyce hadn't planned a wedding in four years—since Tori's accident. Retirement had been on her radar, but far in the future. Helping her daughter recover had brought her career to a halt early, but Joyce thought she'd get to plan one more wedding: Tori's.

The fact that her daughter ended up as straight as they come amused and somewhat baffled her—Tori had been raised by romantically-paired gay dads and a non-romantically-paired lesbian mother living in a queerplatonic relationship you'd be hard pressed to find anywhere else in their tiny town. But Joyce had looked forward to planning Tori and Burt's wedding anyway. Until the day the two of them had sat her down for tea and told her they never planned on getting married.

"I don't really see the point of it," Tori had said. "Why do I have to sign a contract to say I love someone? That makes it seem so bureaucratic. No, thank you."

At first, Joyce had felt like a failure. How had she raised such a cynical daughter? Someone who didn't want to marry the love of their life? But Joyce was likely biased because of her profession, and Tori had every right to stay unmarried.

The more difficult challenge was coming to terms with how she'd never plan another wedding when she'd dreamed of Tori's for decades.

So when Eleanor called, Joyce knew this was it. *This* was the last wedding she'd ever plan. Eleanor and Minnie, Eleanor's fiancée, had visited Joyce the previous year on their trip to Scotland. It was a bit of shock to see Eleanor again; they'd been best friends over a decade ago, before Eleanor's wife had passed away. Eleanor had withdrawn after that, but Joyce had never quite accepted that her friend was lost to her. She was glad she'd clung to hope.

Now she could travel to Juniper Creek, plan the wedding of Eleanor and Minnie's dreams, then come home satisfied that everything was right in the world.

The front door of Joyce's house was unlocked, as usual, and Will's and Andrew's voices floated from the kitchen as she hung up her coat. She smoothed back the wisps of dyed-blond hair that had escaped her bun, then went to get herself a cuppa.

Will and Andrew sat beside each other at the kitchen table, holding hands and looking at something on Andrew's laptop. They shifted their gaze to her as she moved into the room.

"Did you go to Tori's again?" Andrew asked, disapproval plain in his tone.

She raised her chin in defiance. "Maybe."

In typical Andrew fashion, he crossed his arms and somehow looked down his nose at her even though he was sitting and she was standing. Every time he did that, Joyce could see Tori in him so clearly. She may have been adopted, but her expressions were all Andrew. "Joyce, you know you need to give her space. You're going to start a row."

She sighed and turned on the kettle. Over the years, she'd learned that making tea was as much a deflection opportunity as it was a comfort activity. Except Andrew got up and moved to stand beside her. Damn that man and his persistence.

"I'm not going to start a row," she said, not looking at him. "For god's sake, I'm not doing anything wrong. I just thought I'd drop off one more loaf of bread before I leave this weekend, that's all."

Andrew opened his mouth to say more, but Will broke in. "Leave it, Andy. It's not worth it."

She knew without looking that Andrew shook his head. A chair scratched lightly against the kitchen tiles, and she heard

Andrew settle into it, the wood creaking slightly beneath his weight.

No one said a word as Joyce poured each of them a cup of tea. She kept her eyes averted as she handed out the mugs, then she sat at the opposite end of the table from Andrew. The two of them faced each other while Will sat an equal distance between them as if he were a referee. "She says hello, by the way," she said.

"Well, hello back to her." Will pushed his glasses up onto his head. He tapped his fingers on the table, a sign that he was nervous.

A few seconds passed, then Andrew said, "In all seriousness, though, how are you feeling about your trip? You've been coddling Tori more than usual this week." Tea wasn't going to be enough of a distraction tonight, obviously. Andrew had always been too good at reading her, even if she'd known Will for a few years longer.

She cleared her throat. A fraction of the truth wouldn't hurt. "I'm nervous about leaving Tori alone for the tours this season."

Andrew's expression barely changed, and Will said, "JoJo, she's been giving plenty of tours on her own now for a few months. She's seeing her therapist less too."

"Well, yes, but—"

"She'll be fine," Andrew cut in. "We've talked about this. And even if she needs help, we'll be here."

Joyce huffed out a breath, but when she spoke next, her voice was quiet, soft. No point in hiding her feelings, really. "I want to plan Eleanor's wedding. I do. But I've never been away from Tori, or from you two"—she glanced from Andrew to Will, then at the table—"for so long before. I want to be there to make the wedding planning easier. But . . . it's hard to leave."

"Oh, JoJo." Will reached out and covered her hand with his. She flipped her palm over and squeezed his fingers, grateful for the gesture. Andrew always saw more than she wanted him to, but Will knew how to make her feel better. "That's alright. Everyone misses their family when they go away. We'll miss you too. But after everything that's happened between us and Eleanor, you need to do this. Right?" Will and Andrew had been Eleanor's friends as much as she had.

She nodded, tears rising in her eyes.

"And we'll fly in for the wedding—all of us. Tori too. Maybe she'll even bring Burt." Joyce laughed and Andrew snorted; none of them were particularly fond of Burt and his penchant for golf. But Tori liked him, so there it was.

"I'm acting like a child, I know."

"It's alright." Will squeezed her hand. "You've been preparing for the wedding since Eleanor asked you anyway, so I'm sure it'll be easy."

"I hope so." With a sigh of surrender, she pulled her hand from Will's and reached for the laptop. "I want to check my flight time again."

Andrew slid the laptop out of her range, and Will raised a hand. "Ah, since we have you here, we'd like to talk about something."

Andrew moved his eyebrows in a way that indicated his agreement and signaled for her to stay calm at the same time. Amazing what that man could express with his eyebrows.

The nervous feeling in Joyce's stomach grew like a balloon in her chest. "Okay." She clutched her mug, holding it firmly on the table in front of her as if it could shield her from whatever came next.

"It's not bad, JoJo, I promise," Will said, his eyes lighting up. "Remember how, before we started the business, we talked about how we'd like to retire in Italy?"

"Yes." She drew out the word, her mind already connecting the dots.

"Well, you've already retired, and you know that Andy and I have been considering doing the same for a few months now. We're getting on in years, as you know, and it's not as easy or enjoyable to be out on the water all the time."

"Yes," she repeated. She'd been part of those conversations, urging them to take it easy now that they were financially set for a comfortable future. "Do you think Tori's ready to take over?"

"I think she is," Andrew said, and Will nodded. "She's taken over the tours, and she's got her own place now. She's got Burt, and she's doing well."

"Alright. So . . . ?"

"So, how do you feel about looking into moving to Italy?" Andrew asked.

"Italy." Joyce breathed out the word. They had talked about it many times, and they'd even gone there for vacation when Tori was a toddler. But then their wildlife tour business had taken off, as had Joyce's wedding-planning business. And Tori had grown up and found Burt. Italy had become a sort of pipe dream for Joyce—something that could be fun, but she never thought would happen. It was a dream, not a reality. "You truly want to move there?"

"Wouldn't it be nice to sail in warmer water for once?" Will went on. "Maybe the boat wouldn't be ours, not in the same way, but we'd still be by the water and—"

"And there's no reason not to, really," Andrew said.

Will ran a hand through his gray hair in his excitement, leaning forward. "Exactly. What do you think, JoJo?"

"I . . . I think we've wanted to go back there for a while."

"I hear a *but*," Will said, his brow furrowing.

"But"—she swallowed, hard—"I need . . . I need to think about it." An image of Italy popped into her mind, cerulean water stretching from rows of houses built on massive hillsides. She could easily see herself standing on the beach with Will and Andrew, their feet in the water. But Tori wouldn't be there.

"Of course," Andrew said. "Take the time you need. We don't have to decide anything right away."

But they would need to decide eventually.

Joyce stood, her body feeling extra heavy somehow. "I'm rather tired, so I think I'll head to bed. Goodnight, you two."

As she walked up to her room one step at a time, Will's gentle voice floated to her from the kitchen. "Maybe this was a bad time to bring up Italy."

It wasn't until Joyce had changed into her flannel pajamas, put her hearing aids on the charger, and buried herself under the covers that she realized she'd left her full cup of tea sitting on the kitchen table.

CHAPTER THREE

LORETTA

91 DAYS UNTIL THE WEDDING

*L*oretta sat outside in the chicken enclosure, her girls pecking around her ankles. She'd given them scraps from a squash she'd eaten the day before, and they seemed to enjoy it. The fresh air and the familiar sounds of clucking helped take her mind off the wedding-planning dinner that night. Part of Loretta wanted to ask Evvie to join her, Joyce, Eleanor, and Minnie, but Loretta needed to stand on her own two feet. No matter how unprepared she felt, she would move forward and figure out her next steps as she went. Hopefully without tripping.

Loretta arrived at The June Bug twenty minutes early. Her entire life had been like that—getting where she needed to be before anyone else, then sitting in silence and trying to look busy. Today, she'd brought her sketchbook with her, mostly to distract herself from brooding while she waited. She made herself comfortable at one of the booths and pulled out her sketching supplies, using a succulent on the decorative wall dividing the booths as her subject.

"Good evening," Jamie, the diner's owner said, chipper as ever. "Can I get you something to drink?"

"Water, please."

Jamie nodded and headed toward the kitchen.

For the next few minutes, Loretta tried to lose herself in her work, in the scratch of her pencil on the page and the feel of the paper under her hand.

A murmur of approaching voices caught her attention. She looked up to see Minnie and Eleanor walking toward her booth with another woman who must have been Joyce. Reluctantly, Loretta slid her sketchbook in her bag and tried to look presentable.

In the past few days, she hadn't thought much about Joyce, but she doubted she would have pictured the businesslike woman before her now. Her entire outfit and way of holding herself contrasted Eleanor so strongly. Where Eleanor wore long, flowy clothing, Joyce wore a gray skirt, a bright pink blazer, and heels that clicked on the floor. *Heels*, at their age! And Joyce's poise made Loretta's back sore just looking at her, whereas Eleanor always moved as if she were dancing. Joyce practically *shone* with confidence, and Loretta couldn't help but be drawn to her light.

"Hello," Minnie said as she slid into the seat across from Loretta.

"Hi," Loretta replied, the word coming out quieter than she wanted.

Eleanor slid in next to Minnie. "Loretta, wonderful to see you. This is Joyce, the friend and wedding planner I told you about."

Joyce held out her hand, continuing with the business vibe. "Nice to meet you," she said, grasping Loretta's hand firmly. Loretta's pulse skittered at the feeling of Joyce's skin against hers; something about this woman and her bright smile had kicked Loretta's nerves into high gear.

"You as well." Loretta forced strength into her voice.

Joyce slid into the booth beside Loretta, her feet crossed at the ankles, her back straight. Hadn't she arrived in town only the day before? Maybe jet lag didn't affect her—she seemed like the type of person who would smile her way through anything.

"What can I get you ladies to drink?" Jamie asked, setting down Loretta's water. As the other women ordered—iced tea for Minnie, ginger beer for Eleanor, and coffee for Joyce—Loretta sipped her water as daintily as she could. The last thing she needed was to spill all over herself and make a bad impression in front of the unexpectedly attractive wedding planner.

The four of them exchanged small talk for a few minutes, which made Loretta's skin itch. She said as little as possible, *hmming* a few times to give the impression that talking about the weather and airplane food engaged her.

After Jamie took their orders, Eleanor said, "Joyce, we took a tour the other day of Loretta's farm and the barn where we're getting married, and it's a delightful area. I think you're going to love it."

Loretta wasn't so sure. She fought the urge to glance over Joyce's outfit again, trying to imagine how she'd walk on the grass with those heels. She'd probably sink right in and become part of the decor, like a fancy business lawn gnome.

Joyce smiled again, revealing crow's feet by her eyes that softened her face. "It doesn't matter if *I* love it. What matters is what *you* think. It's my job to make sure you both get your dream wedding."

The sincerity in her tone calmed Loretta somewhat. It reminded her that Minnie and Eleanor's wedding sat at the center of this dinner. Joyce probably wouldn't even pay much attention to her.

"We should talk about that," Joyce continued, pulling a notebook and a pen out of her purse. Not your regular school notebook either, but a sturdy thing with a pale-pink-and-white swirly cover and a gold coil. The pen matched. Loretta leaned over slightly and saw notes in neat handwriting cascading down the page. "Eleanor, over the phone you told me that you'd had a look around already, and nothing felt right to you. What type of wedding *does* feel right?"

Loretta sat up straighter. Her business revolved around her clients' wants and needs, and she didn't know what those were beyond the basics. Every client would be different, of course, but Minnie and Eleanor could give her a few clues about how to tailor her marketing. That part of her business still had her floundering.

As if she knew which times were convenient to break up the conversation, Jamie came over with their food balanced on a tray. Loretta had ordered vegetarian pasta, Joyce had ordered a chicken Caesar salad, and Minnie and Eleanor had both ordered burgers.

"We want a smaller wedding," Minnie said as she put ketchup on her plate for her fries. "Not tiny, but nothing huge."

Joyce speared lettuce on her fork then turned to Loretta. "How many people will fit inside the barn?"

A piece of pasta chose that moment to get stuck in Loretta's throat. She coughed and sipped her water, Joyce's gaze burning holes in her face. "We can comfortably fit one hundred fifty, maybe two hundred if needed."

Minnie let out a sound halfway between a laugh and a choke. "I don't think we'll need that much seating."

Joyce nodded once, seeming satisfied. "Have you made a guest list?"

Loretta tried to focus on the details as the three of them talked, but the longer the conversation went on, the more she wondered if she really needed to be there. They discussed the guest list, cake flavors, flowers—which Minnie and Eleanor would provide from their own shops—and food. None of it sparked any inspiration for how Loretta could decorate the barn or create her brand image, and she couldn't give any valuable input at this stage of the planning.

Not to mention Joyce's intense focus on every point of discussion. Her hand flew over her notebook as she jotted down what seemed like more than Minnie and Eleanor said, and she nodded so much, Loretta wondered if her neck hurt.

"What about the overall aesthetic?" Joyce asked.

That drew Loretta's attention again; the wedding aesthetic tied closely to the venue.

Minnie and Eleanor looked at each other and smiled. If love were visible, it'd likely float between them in the air, maybe as little pink hearts or a sparkly mist.

"We have a Sunflower Festival here every year," Minnie said. "I've been planning it for years, and last year Eleanor helped me, along with our friends. It was a special event for us, and we'd like our wedding to feel similar."

Loretta could work with that. She'd been to the Sunflower Festival many times, and she could already see how the summer festival could translate to wedding decor. Strings of lights, flowers, burlap ribbon, wooden chairs and tables . . . She felt foolish for not thinking of it before.

"With different flowers, though," Minnie said. "We'd like to have peonies as our central flower, rather than sunflowers."

"Oh!" Joyce clapped, bright-eyed. "Peonies are my favorite! What color?"

Eleanor's eyes twinkled at her friend's enthusiasm. "White and pink, most likely."

"What do you think, Loretta?" Joyce asked, her eyebrows lifted, her smile reaching her blue eyes.

It was only the second time Joyce had addressed her directly since her greeting, and Loretta felt oddly in the spotlight. "I think that's a wonderful idea. It'll work perfectly."

She hoped her words sounded enthusiastic enough, and they must have because Joyce beamed at her.

A fluttering sensation filled Loretta's stomach, and the anxiety she'd felt throughout the meal so far lifted slightly. As they continued to talk, she found herself wondering how she could make Joyce smile like that again.

CHAPTER FOUR

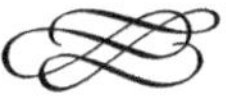

JOYCE

Joyce enjoyed what she'd experienced of Juniper Creek so far. Eleanor had pointed out a few things on their drive in the previous day—the wooden sign that read "Welcome to Juniper Creek" in cheery yellow letters, Minnie's and Eleanor's shops on Main Street, the bookstore (also on Main Street), the library, and the diner they currently sat in. The place held a similar charm as Stonehaven, Scotland, where Eleanor lived before she moved to Canada. When Eleanor pointed out their similarities, her face practically glowed, and Joyce thought she understood part of why Eleanor seemed so happy.

Even the B&B acting as Joyce's temporary home oozed with the sweetness often found in small tourist towns. The Bluebell sat just down the street from the diner and the library, right at town center. The couple who owned it, Dean and Olivia, went out of their way to welcome her and make sure she had everything she needed. They'd taken the inn's theme to its farthest reach, with differently patterned blue wallpaper in every room.

Despite the loudness of the colors, Joyce had slept so heavily on Friday night that she hadn't gotten up to use the loo, which was unusual for her. She'd even slept in, which was also unusual. Part of her wondered if her total unconsciousness had come from the jet lag or from her stress over Will and Andrew's proposal to move to Italy.

She hadn't been able to stop thinking about it, not even when the two of them had dropped her off at Edinburgh airport and hugged her goodbye. Will had kissed her forehead and said to call if she needed anything, and Andrew had warned her to drink plenty of water because the food on the plane was salty and would make her feet swell. That bloody man was always taking care of her.

At least when Eleanor had picked her up after breakfast that morning, Joyce had had something else to focus on. Eleanor had taken her to see Vera and Kat, Eleanor's daughter and grandchild. They'd both grown up so much, Joyce barely recognized them. Especially Kat, whom she'd met as a toddler, but had only seen photos of since then.

On their way to the diner, Eleanor had told her they were meeting Loretta there. "She's the owner of the barn. I hope you don't mind, but I offered your help with setting up her business."

The idea of helping someone start a wedding-related business filled Joyce with energy. She never turned down an opportunity to help someone else in the industry. "Oh, I'd love to!"

Eleanor shot her a fond grin. "I thought you would. Loretta didn't exactly say yes to the idea, but maybe you can talk about it tonight."

And now, at dinner, Joyce was fully in wedding-planning mode. Eleanor may have been her friend, but she was also a client. No matter how distracted Joyce felt, she would make Eleanor and Minnie's dream wedding come to life. That's what she was here for, after all.

"So, we've got peonies and a rustic barn to work with. That's a good start," Joyce said, nodding over her notebook.

Joyce glanced at Loretta, who'd been quiet throughout the entire dinner. Eleanor had told Joyce a bit about Loretta in their earlier conversation. She was also in her seventies, she lived on a farm outside of town, she owned chickens, and her brother used to be in a rock band. For some reason, Joyce had expected Loretta to be livelier. Maybe the rock band comment had given her the wrong idea.

In reality, Loretta was almost sullen, her smiles small and brief. Something about her tugged at Joyce, though, like there was more to Loretta than she showed the world.

Joyce drew her eyes away from the venue owner and back to her notebook. Her brain was packed full of plans to make various lists in her phone and set reminders for certain tasks in the coming weeks. "You said you'd been looking at vendors, but you hadn't found anyone you wanted to book with, right? Why is that?"

Eleanor and Minnie glanced at each other, unspoken words passing between them in the same way Joyce, Will, and Andrew often communicated.

"I wanted to see what was available," Eleanor said. "There are so many wonderful vendors in the area."

Minnie cleared her throat. "But I already had an idea of who we should book with. I've established connections with a few vendors from the Sunflower Festival, and there are so many people in town we can employ. I don't see the need to look elsewhere."

Ah, yes. The first glimmer of conflict. No matter how much two people loved each other, a disagreement inevitably cropped up during wedding planning. The pressure to get everything perfect, to bring a specific vision to life on such a big day, could overwhelm the most level-headed person. Joyce had seen it more than once.

"You never know what's out there if you don't look," Eleanor said.

Minnie sighed. "But we did look."

"I know." Eleanor wrapped an arm around Minnie's waist and drew her close. "We did look. And none of them felt right because *you* are right, my darling. We should involve the people we know and love. That's why I brought Joyce along."

A subtle heat shot to Joyce's cheeks, and she tried not to smile too much.

"And that's why we booked at the farm," Eleanor added. "Not to mention how ideal it is for us."

"Speaking of the farm," Joyce said, shifting her attention to Loretta, "would you mind if I looked at it tomorrow? I'd love to see the space and get a better idea of what we're working with."

Loretta turned to face her, pushing aside a strand of her dark hair. Joyce wished her hair had maintained its color like that, but of course it hadn't. Now she dyed it every few weeks to hide her gray roots. She had the shockingly bold urge to run her hands through Loretta's hair and see if it was as thick as it looked.

"Sure," Loretta replied. "What time would you like to come over?"

Joyce pulled her gaze away from Loretta's curls. "That depends on Eleanor, I'm afraid. I'll need a ride."

Eleanor frowned. "Minnie and I both work tomorrow, unfortunately, unless we go in the evening."

"You're not renting a car while you're here?" Loretta asked, the question void of judgement.

Joyce held up a hand. "No, thank you. I barely drive at home, and at least I know which side to drive on there." Her dislike for cars hadn't caused many problems in the UK since you could travel most places by train. As far as she knew, Canada had a much different transit culture, though.

Loretta shifted and pulled her gray cardigan tighter around her. The sleeves were so long, they covered most of her hands. "I could pick you up, if you want."

"You wouldn't mind?" Joyce hadn't expected the offer, considering how withdrawn Loretta seemed.

"No." Loretta shrugged.

"Well, then I'll take you up on that." Joyce didn't want to dump herself on Eleanor's family, and she didn't fancy sitting in the Bluebell all day while Minnie and Eleanor worked, no matter how hospitable the owners were. "Maybe I can even give you a few business tips while I'm there."

"Maybe." Loretta's tone was so cryptic, Joyce couldn't tell

what that meant. Was that a I-want-your-help-but-have-trouble-asking *maybe*? Or a get-off-my-lawn *maybe*? She supposed she'd figure it out eventually.

"What time works best for you?"

Loretta pursed her lips as she thought. "Is nine o'clock too early? I'm always up before seven to feed the girls."

"The girls?"

"She's got chickens," Eleanor said. "Named after goddesses."

Joyce's interest piqued. "Goddesses? I'll make sure to dress appropriately to meet them. And nine works for me." She jotted the time in her notebook and added a reminder to her phone to be safe. "I'm an early riser as well, at home. I'm hoping to rise early here too, once I shake off the jet lag."

"Perfect." Eleanor looked around at them all. "Now that's sorted. Do we need to go over anything else this evening?"

Everyone had finished their meals, besides a few fries lingering on Minnie's plate and the tomatoes Joyce had pulled from her salad. For the last few years, tomatoes had upset her stomach.

"We could go over the other vendors you'd like to use," Joyce said, "or you can make a list, and we can go through them another time. There's no rush." There was, in fact, a slight rush. They only had until June—three months—to plan the entire wedding. But Joyce always aimed to avoid stressing out her clients more than they needed to be. Especially when those clients were also close friends.

"Great." Minnie yawned. "I had a terrible sleep last night, and I wouldn't mind tucking in early."

"Is that alright?" Eleanor asked Joyce. "I don't know how much you were hoping to accomplish today, but I feel like we didn't do much of anything."

"We did enough." Joyce snapped her notebook shut. "Why don't you email me a list of the vendors you're considering, and we'll go from there?"

Eleanor looked at Minnie, who nodded.

The four of them paid then left the diner. The sun had gone

down already, leaving the evening air chilly and damp. The smell of rain reminded Joyce of Scotland, her heart squeezing painfully at the thought of Will and Andrew at home with their feet up on the coffee table watching some comedy show. And of Tori on the boat, her hair whipping in the wind.

Joyce patted her own hair, still neatly in its bun. "Goodnight," she said, hugging both Eleanor and Minnie. Loretta stood behind them, and Joyce's instincts told her to hug Loretta next, even though she barely knew the woman. Loretta kept her distance, though, her hands tucked into her oversized cardigan sleeves. "See you tomorrow?"

Loretta nodded and gave her a polite smile. Joyce couldn't see the details of her face beneath the shadow cast from the diner's front light. "Nine o'clock. Have a good sleep." Loretta waved then turned to walk down the sidewalk, presumably to her car.

Joyce watched her go. The woman was like a mystery waiting to be uncovered, and Joyce would happily play the detective, if only to make sure the wedding went smoothly.

As she walked back to the Bluebell, she found herself looking forward to visiting the farm. To scouting out Minnie and Eleanor's wedding venue, to meeting hens named after goddesses, and to learning more about the quiet woman she felt inexplicably curious about.

CHAPTER FIVE

LORETTA

As Loretta said her goodbyes, she became more antsy to get home and work on her business. Joyce seemed happy enough to help, but Loretta wanted to do as much as she could by herself.

She sat at her kitchen table with her laptop in front of her, trying to decide what to work on. Her eyes fell on the portrait she'd drawn of a wedding in town two years ago; she kept it with her as she worked on her business to remind herself of her goals. Of her *why*. She hadn't been to the wedding, but she'd seen the happy couple emerge from the church on a sunny day, laughing and holding hands.

In that moment, as she'd watched them gaze at each other as if no one else existed, something had snapped in her brain. She was done with being stuck in the fog. She wanted that kind of joy in her own life, even if she hadn't known at the time how to get it.

She'd had her own bubble of happiness once with Gail, but that bubble had popped. They'd split after being together for two decades. Loretta had realized that she'd been mistaken, that the person she thought she knew was on a different wavelength altogether. That she'd wasted years and emotions and dreams with Gail, and none of that had meant anything.

A memory surfaced of when she'd last seen Gail. The two of them had stood in their apartment, Loretta's bags at her feet.

"Let me say goodbye," Gail had said, reaching for Loretta's arm.

Loretta had pulled back, her throat tight with tears. "No. I . . . I'd rather not." She'd never been good at goodbyes, and she'd been in too much pain from what Gail had said to her the night before.

She'd left Gail standing by the door, and she hadn't looked back to see her ex-girlfriend's expression. She hadn't wanted to see it—to remember the pain on her face. Or maybe the lack of pain, a sign that she'd been ready to let go of Loretta for a while.

Loretta hadn't been ready to let go. When she'd told Gail she needed to move back home to help her mother on the farm, she'd had no doubt Gail would follow. It might have taken time for Gail to get her things in order, to quit her job in California and find a new one in British Columbia, but Loretta thought she'd do it. So they could stay together, like they'd always talked about— supporting each other through thick and thin.

She'd been wrong.

With a shuddering breath, Loretta pulled herself back to the present, the portrait of the wedding still on the table beside her laptop.

Darkness had fully descended outside, and she still needed to feed the girls. She also needed their presence for her own peace of mind.

Before Matthias lived with her, her hens had been her best friends, and they still listened with an attentive ear whenever she needed to rant. At least, that's what she told herself. In reality, they cared more about the food, but they needed her to give it to them.

"Hello, my lovelies," she said as she sprinkled chicken feed on the ground. Her nose ran slightly in the cold, and she wondered if the girls would need their heater tonight. It wasn't quite spring yet, although a sense of renewal permeated the air.

She sat on a stool inside the chicken wire, reaching to pet the goddesses when they got close. She ran her hands through her hair and tilted her neck side to side, stretching it. The silhouette of the barn caught her eye, and she shook her head, thinking back to dinner. "What made me think I could open a business, hm?" she asked her girls, who pecked at the ground around her feet. The soft ruffle of their feathers comforted her. "I know nothing about entrepreneurship, and next to nothing about weddings."

She could count the number of weddings she'd been to on one hand, and—obviously—she'd never had her own. "How am I supposed to help people have the wedding of their dreams when I couldn't even keep my own partner?" With a body-emptying sigh, she hung her head in her hands, not caring if dirt got in her hair.

The idea to turn the barn into a wedding venue had come to her on a walk one day. She'd stopped in the barn doorway, looking at the disintegrating boards and inhaling the musty air. She always carried her sketchbook with her, just in case, and she'd had the strongest urge to sketch the barn as something transformed.

She'd been thinking about how many people in Juniper Creek had been falling in love recently: Minnie and Eleanor, the librarian and her childhood best friend, her brother and Evvie, and those people who got married two years before. Loretta hadn't been able to shake the image of pure joy on all their faces.

Before she'd known it, she'd brought to life a scene of the barn fully renovated with chandeliers overhead, long tables laid out and set with floral centerpieces, a wedding cake on display in the background.

Although she couldn't find joy through romance for herself anymore, she wanted to do her damnedest to help create happily-ever-afters for other people.

But now here she was, struggling to convince herself that she could do this. That she could make the barn worthy of weddings and bring people there to find happiness. She pictured Joyce walking into the diner with pep in her step and groaned.

Loretta was not the type of person to light up someone's day. Her mother had always said, "Your sweet punim will get stuck that way" every time Loretta frowned, which was often. Although she tried to be more aware of her resting bitch face now, it didn't bode well for her starting a person-facing business.

But Loretta knew what the opposite of joy looked like, and steering well clear of that would help her. Plus, she championed romance.

As long as the romance wasn't hers.

As usual, the next day Loretta got up early to feed the girls. She completed her chores then settled into her living room recliner to sketch and quiet her mind until she had to leave to pick up Joyce.

She let her hand move across a page in her sketchbook without thinking about what she drew, wanting to get lost in the art. Her timer went off at eight-thirty—time to get going—so she set down her pencil.

She'd drawn a woman's face, the lines soft. A slightly upturned nose, high cheekbones, a small cleft in her chin, her lips full. Loretta blinked and frowned. The portrait looked kind of like Joyce. With a shake of her head, Loretta threw the sketchbook on the side table and went to get her shoes on.

Juniper Creek felt sleepy this morning, maybe because of the cool weather. Not to mention, the shops on Main Street didn't open until ten on Sundays instead of their usual nine. Loretta didn't have to fight any traffic, and she pulled up at the Bluebell ten minutes early. She hadn't thought to get Joyce's phone number the night before, so she'd have to go inside to get her.

She smoothed her jeans—as if that'd make them any neater—and patted her hair where it frizzed. No time like the present.

A tiny bell jingled over the front door as Loretta let herself in. She expected to see Olivia behind the welcome desk, but it was empty. The smell of bacon wafted through the air, making

Loretta wrinkle her nose. She'd never seen the appeal of bacon; she hadn't eaten it growing up, and then she'd gone vegetarian in her twenties.

With no one there to greet her, Loretta floundered. Should she wait for Joyce here? Should she go look for her? She turned to the foyer, where two couches sat across from each other with a wood-and-stone coffee table in between, and found her answer.

Joyce sat on one of the couches, her laptop on her lap, consulting her pink notebook. A poster board stood propped on the table in front of her. Her outfit fell more into the business casual category today: black slacks, and a navy blouse with a white Peter Pan collar.

Loretta approached the couch and cleared her throat softly. Joyce looked up, her blue eyes locking on Loretta's. "Good morning," Loretta said, smiling in a way she hoped appeared friendly even though it felt like a grimace.

She held her emotions in check this morning, but that didn't ease her nerves about showing Joyce the farm.

"Good morning." Joyce looked at her watch, a small round face with a thin black strap. "You're early."

Loretta shrugged. "I like to be punctual."

"Well, I appreciate that." Joyce smiled at her, all warmth. "Would you like to see the start of the wedding board?" She beckoned Loretta over.

"Sure." Loretta wanted to ask what a wedding board was, but she didn't want to give away her lack of knowledge.

The wedding board became obvious, anyway, as she moved behind the couch to peer over Joyce's shoulder at the display. In the day and a half she'd been in town, Joyce had somehow made a board with a burlap base, and she'd pinned a few photos to it: one of Minnie and Eleanor in front of a glowing arch, smiling at each other as Minnie slid a ring on Eleanor's finger; one showing a bouquet of pink and white peonies; and one with a barn painted white and lit up from within with thousands of lights.

Loretta's barn currently looked nothing like that. Gerard and

Landon, Juniper Creek's father-and-son construction duo, had replaced the rotting boards and made sure the structure met safety standards, but the walls were bare, and wires hung where light fixtures would go. They still had to replace a few boards in the loft, which would eventually serve as a ceremony space if clients wanted to have their ceremony indoors.

"What do you think?" Joyce asked, and Loretta realized she'd been waiting for a reaction.

"It looks exactly like what Minnie and Eleanor talked about," Loretta said. *And nothing like my barn. Yet.*

Joyce put her hands on her knees, staring at the board with pride. "I'm glad you think so. I'll keep adding to it as we plan, and I'll give it to them as a gift when we're finished."

That was the type of thing Loretta needed to consider: client gifts. If gifts were standard in the wedding industry, Loretta needed to figure out how to put together baskets or something for her clients. She wished there was an instruction manual for budding wedding businesses.

"That's a good idea," she told Joyce. "I'm sure they'll love it." Joyce nodded and began cleaning up. "Can I help with anything?"

Joyce swept a few pens into a bag then slid her laptop into a smart-looking briefcase. "No, I'll only be a mo'."

While Joyce finished packing her things, Loretta reached into her purse and surreptitiously pulled out a ginger chew. She could always rely on ginger to calm her stomach, and at the sight of Joyce's wedding board, a subtle wave of nausea had rolled through her.

"Ready," Joyce said. She'd slid on a black trench coat and now stood in front of Loretta, the wedding board tucked under her arm.

"Alright. The car's this way." Loretta cringed at herself as she walked outside. *The car's this way?* She sounded like a chauffeur.

She'd parked right out front, so they didn't have far to walk. Loretta's car had served her well for years, even with the rust spots over the wheel wells.

For a second, she almost reached for the passenger-side door to hold it open for Joyce, but she thought better of it. Without a word, Joyce put her things in the back then settled beside Loretta in the passenger seat.

"It's going to take some getting used to—being on this side of the car," Joyce said.

Loretta thought back to Joyce's comment about not driving here. "Ah yes, the *right* side."

Joyce quirked an eyebrow. "Who made you the judge of right and wrong?"

"I'm not about to get blasphemous here."

"Well, I'll defer to you on this one since you've got goddesses on your side." Joyce's voice hid a laugh. "But that won't always be the case."

"You don't think so?" Loretta was impressed Joyce remembered about her chickens' names.

"A person can't always be right."

"Unless they are a goddess."

"Well, sure, but you're only *associated* with a few. Unless you're not telling me something."

Loretta suppressed a smile. She hadn't meant to imply she *was* a goddess, but she'd take it. "You'll never know."

Despite her nerves around Joyce, Loretta fell into banter with her easily and the ride to the farm proved less awkward than Loretta had anticipated. Joyce told her Dean had made her a full Scottish breakfast, and she asked more about Loretta's hens. The more Loretta talked about her girls, the more comfortable she became.

"This is the farm," she said as they parked. The sky had brightened overhead, no clouds in sight. A rain-free day meant a mud-free path, and Loretta couldn't ask for more. She glanced at Joyce's feet—no heels today, thank goodness. "Would you like to see the barn first? Or we could walk around the grounds?"

"Do you mind if I drop my things inside? Then I'd like to

walk around. And I'd love to meet your hens, if they're currently accepting company."

A smile stole over Loretta's face. Maybe showing Joyce around wouldn't be so bad.

CHAPTER SIX

JOYCE

*J*oyce couldn't remember the last time she'd been to a farm. Most of her clients had their weddings at event centers, castles, or churches, not in barns. But she knew from her research that barn weddings had grown in popularity over the past few years in North America.

Loretta's farm fell firmly in the cute category, but it needed work. The road in wasn't paved, though a dirt road could add a sense of charm. She tried to picture the scene as they drove up it—where the cars would park, where the guests would walk to reach the ceremony and the reception. The yard was overgrown, but the house itself was a picture of country sweetness: one story with a covered front porch, wooden patio furniture and a porch swing, blue siding with white trim.

Joyce followed Loretta to the front door, her briefcase in one hand and her other holding the wedding board. Her gaze fell on a small box affixed to the right side of the doorframe at about eye level. "What's this?" she asked, nodding to it.

Loretta glanced over her shoulder. "Hm? Oh, a mezuzah. Our family is Jewish."

"Sorry, what's it called again?" Joyce hadn't heard of that before.

"A mezuzah. It's basically a decorative case with a prayer or scripture inside it. We had the same one up for years, but the weather wore it down. My mother replaced it a couple years before she passed." The softness of Loretta's face reflected the fondness in her voice. "I keep it up as a reminder of her."

"That's sweet." Joyce hadn't been close to her own mother. She'd been the second youngest of eight kids, and neither of her parents had paid much attention to her. With that many siblings —and a staunchly Catholic family—she'd learned to fight for what she wanted.

She only hoped she'd given Tori enough care over the years that she'd look at something of Joyce's one day with that fond expression.

As soon as Joyce stepped inside Loretta's house, the subtle scent of lavender washed over her, making her feel oddly at home. The house had a simple layout: an attached living room and kitchen with a hallway branching to the right that presumably led to the bedrooms and a loo or two. Joyce glimpsed a tiled room across the house at the back door that was likely the laundry room. Although simple, the space was roomy—much larger than Joyce, Will, and Andrew's house—which seemed typical of North American homes.

Two gray couches sat kitty-corner in the living room next to a worn wooden coffee table, all of it muted in the same way Loretta seemed to be. But even with the furniture, Joyce could tell there was history there, in the one couch cushion more broken in than the rest, in the scuff marks on the coffee table-top. A small TV perched on a shelf across from one of the couches, and a recliner rested next to a side table closer to the back door. The walls held a few framed photos that Joyce ached to get a better look at, and a piece of circular abstract art hung over a quaint bookshelf. The bright green and yellow paint seemed oddly joyful and modern in comparison to the rest of the space.

"You've got a nice place," Joyce said, still looking around. A few green plants scattered on shelves and the kitchen windowsill brought a sense of life and growth.

"Thanks." Loretta slipped her shoes off, so Joyce followed suit. "You can put your things on the table, if you like. I'm going to run to the washroom."

Joyce set her bag on a kitchen chair and put the board on the table. Even the kitchen had a classic farmhouse feel with the rotating wooden mug holder, the tea towels with bees and plants on them, and the kettle sitting ready on the stovetop. It softened how she'd viewed Loretta's quietness.

The faint sound of clucking reached Joyce's ears, and she followed it to the back window. The chicken coop sat just meters from the house with two hens walking around their little yard. A thrill shot through Joyce. The goddesses! She'd never been so intrigued with chickens before, but these ones had a reputation.

She grabbed her boots and put them by the back door, then she watched the hens as she waited for Loretta. If she leaned to the right, the barn came into view. It looked more rundown than she'd expected, but maybe it'd be nicer upon closer inspection. At least the yard spanned a large area, definitely enough to host a wedding. The field would likely be full of wildflowers soon as well, and that would make for a gorgeous backdrop.

Footsteps approached from the hallway, and Loretta said, "I see you've found the girls."

Joyce turned to meet her, smiling sheepishly. "Do you mind if we meet them first?"

"Not at all." Loretta grabbed her shoes and a spiral sketchbook, and before Joyce knew it, they were back outside in the chill March air. "These are my girls," Loretta said, leading Joyce to the coop and the surrounding chicken wire. She opened a door and ushered Joyce inside.

Two more hens had emerged from the coop since Joyce and Loretta came outside, and a fifth stood at the top of the ramp leading to the ground. Sunlight bathed their feathers, and they seemed to revel in the warmth.

"Joyce, meet Athena, Artemis, Persephone, Circe, and Aphrodite." Loretta pointed at each hen in turn as she named them. Joyce would be hard-pressed to remember which was which, though. "You can pet them if you want. They're friendly with people."

"Not with other animals?" Joyce crouched and held her hand toward the nearest hen—Artemis, maybe? The hen cocked her head then turned as if to give Joyce permission to pet her. Joyce ran the backs of her fingers over the hen's reddish-brown feathers, all of which had black tips.

"I haven't tried them with other animals, but they pick on each other sometimes. Persephone gets picked on the most, possibly because she and Circe are Rhode Island Reds while the rest of them are Wyandottes."

"Hmm." Joyce continued petting Artemis, admiring her feathers. "They really are gorgeous birds."

"Thank you." Those words radiated pride, and rightfully so. Joyce doubted she could ever successfully bring up a flock of hens.

They settled into silence for a few minutes until Joyce's ankles hurt. She pushed to standing with a grunt—her joints weren't made for crouching anymore—and turned to see Loretta leaning against the coop, a hen in her arms. Loretta's face was softer, her expression happier than Joyce had seen her yet as she held that chicken, staring out over the field behind the house.

"Shall we take a walk then?" Joyce asked.

"Sure." Loretta put down the hen, who went along pecking at her food, completely unfazed.

As they left the chicken enclosure, Loretta drew her shoulders back. She cleared her throat. "I know the grounds still need work, and so does the barn, but I've got sketches I can show you for what I'm hoping everything will look like in the end." A note of defensiveness rang out in her tone.

Joyce hadn't criticized anything, but she couldn't deny she'd been skeptical when she heard about the wedding timeline. You couldn't transform a barn into a wedding venue overnight, and it took an organized person to get it done properly.

The grounds *did* need work, like Loretta said. Wedding parties would struggle in places where the mud had built up, and guests would need a firmer surface to walk on for the main pathways. Joyce wondered if Loretta had hired a landscaper yet; if not, that needed to go at the top of the priority list.

The barn loomed larger as they approached, and Joyce's opinion improved. While it appeared rundown, that was mostly because of the color than the barn itself. Some of the boards had clearly been replaced, which made it patchy like an oversized wooden quilt.

"Here's the barn." Loretta stopped and opened her arms wide in front of the building as if to encompass it. "There haven't been animals living in it for years, and I made sure it's up to standard. I've got the proper permits and everything, and I got it rewired already so we can put in light fixtures and have plug-ins available."

"I can see you've had people working on it," Joyce said, nodding at a patch of lighter wooden boards. "Can we go inside?"

"Of course." Loretta rolled the barn door open, which moved easily and seemed to be in good shape. It would be a popular wedding feature for sure. "There's no light yet, so watch your step."

Joyce followed her onto what appeared to be a new wooden floor. The building stretched out larger than she'd thought it would, and she pictured tables and chairs filling the space. Wires hung from the ceiling, and if Joyce imagined lights there and the walls painted, she saw the potential. "I can see it," she said quietly; something about the space made her want to speak in hushed tones.

"There's a loft as well. Would you like to see that?"

"I'd love to."

Loretta led her up a set of stairs and into the loft. Like the door, they seemed sturdy and reliable. A few of the steps looked brand new. "This space needs more work." She stepped aside so Joyce could move past her.

Sunlight filtered in through holes in the boards, breaking up the dimness inside. Dust motes danced in the sun rays under the high gabled ceiling, creating an almost mystical scene. Even though this space lacked the finished look of the main room, Joyce could *feel* the potential here. "Oh yes," she said. "I think this would be a gorgeous space for a ceremony."

"Really?" Joyce could have sworn Loretta sighed in relief. "Do you think Minnie and Eleanor could have their ceremony in here? I also want the option for clients to have the ceremony outside."

Joyce nodded thoughtfully. "We can ask them, but either would work. As long as the renovations are finished on time."

"Yes, yes, of course."

Loretta moved farther into the room, her face tilted upward as she walked around. She moved through a beam of sunlight, the golden glow washing over her face and highlighting her eyelashes. She breathed in deeply, relaxing as if the barn air itself centered her. She turned toward Joyce, and Joyce jolted—she'd been caught staring. "Would you like to see my sketches?"

Joyce didn't know Loretta well, but her love for the space and her passion for the project shone clearly on her face. "Yes, please."

The sketchbook Joyce had seen earlier materialized out of Loretta's jacket. How big were her pockets? Shoving that thought aside, Joyce moved toward Loretta until she could see the sketchbook clearly, their arms touching. A soft tingle washed over her skin.

"So, this is what I envision for downstairs."

Joyce's lips parted as she looked at the sketch: a rustic wedding in black and white, elegant and somehow magical. How had Loretta portrayed the light like that? "This is beautiful."

Loretta flipped the page. "And this is sort of how I imagined the loft." In this drawing too, Loretta had caught the essence of the sunbeams shining over guests' heads as a couple walked down an aisle lined with mason jars full of flowers. A faceless figure—

the officiant—waited at the far end in front of a triangle arch accented with greenery.

Impressed, Joyce shook her head. "I don't know how you do that."

Loretta's brow furrowed, and when she turned to Joyce, her eyes caught the sun. They were green with flecks of gold, like sunlight filtering through a forest. "How I do what?"

"Draw like that. It's amazing."

"Oh." Loretta closed the sketchbook and tucked her hair behind her ear. *That hair.* Once again, Joyce had the urge to run her hands through it. "Thanks."

"Did you go to art school?" She must have, to achieve detail like that.

"No, I'm self-taught." Loretta avoided Joyce's gaze, but a smile danced around her lips. "So, you think the barn will work?"

Joyce tore her gaze from Loretta and scanned the loft again. "I do. I'll admit, I had my doubts. But you've convinced me." She tried not to let on that she saw Loretta's smile grow, as if she'd been looking for Joyce's approval. "Are you using your sketches on your website to advertise the space?"

Loretta frowned. "No, I hadn't thought of that. My website isn't up yet."

"If you haven't taken *before* photos yet, you could take a few now and post them. Then you could use your sketches to show your vision for the place, and then take *after* photos when it's done. Everyone loves a good transformation story."

"Hmm." Loretta bit her lip. "That's a good idea."

Joyce grinned. She hadn't achieved success in the wedding business for nothing. "Do you want my help setting up the website?"

"I think I'll be able to do it, but thanks." Loretta's shoulders had crept toward her ears, so Joyce decided to back off.

"Okay, well I'm here if you need me. Can we walk around the grounds more? I'd like to get a better idea of the entire setup. Tell me what you've got in mind for food services and loos."

"Right, so, this is what I'm thinking . . ."

As they exited the barn, the wheels in Joyce's mind turned faster and faster, ideas for Eleanor and Minnie's wedding flooding in. Now that they had secured the venue, the rest of the planning could begin in earnest.

Even if Loretta didn't want Joyce's help with her business, they'd likely see more of each other in the coming months as they worked. Joyce wasn't at all upset about it.

CHAPTER SEVEN

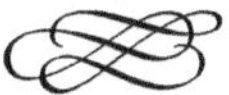

LORETTA

87 DAYS UNTIL THE WEDDING

*L*oretta sat at her kitchen table, staring at her laptop screen and trying not to cry. Building a website? Not a problem. She'd worked in tech for three decades and could understand code. *Designing* said website? She had no idea where to start besides what Joyce had suggested about the photos and sketches, and she wanted to get professional photos taken rather than using her phone. The transformation story made up only one part of the website, though. Loretta needed to consider so much more.

Seven different browser tabs sat open, all of them about marketing in some capacity: color psychology, finding your audience, what to include on your home page, how to set up a newsletter, most effective calls to action, what wedding venues need to offer . . .

At the thought of sifting through all this, she let her head fall forward on her forearms and groaned. Moments like this made her feel like she wasn't cut out to be a business owner. Maybe she should have taken a few online classes before she committed to this, but she couldn't slow down now. She'd already poured the bulk of her savings into the project—it *was* proving more expensive than she'd anticipated.

Minnie and Eleanor's wedding would kick off the business and hopefully bring in other clients. She needed to have the website up and running by their wedding at the very latest.

A knock sounded at the front door, and Loretta lifted her head to see Matthias walk in. She sat up straighter, glad for the distraction. "Hey."

"Hey. What're you up to?"

"Working on my website. Kind of." Yawning, she stretched her arms overhead until her back popped in several places. "What are you doing home?"

"Swapping out clothes and doing laundry." Matthias hefted a duffel bag in front of him. "Since it's warming up, I want more T-shirts."

"Why don't you move in with Evvie officially? You spend almost every night with her anyway, and I barely see you during the day."

He put down the duffel bag and frowned. "Is it . . . okay that I'm over there? I didn't mean to abandon you, and if you want me to spend more time at home, I'll—"

"No, no, that's not what I meant." Loretta shook her head. Had she sounded accusatory? She hadn't meant to, although she didn't love being alone again all the time; it allowed her to sink too far into her head. Plus, she surprisingly enjoyed having Matthias around. "You and Evvie have been together since New Year's, and it seems like a lot of work to cart things back and forth between here and her house."

Matthias crossed his arms. "You're not wrong." He pulled out a chair and sat across from her, leaning back. "I guess I just thought . . . Well, I moved back here to be with you, and you live here. But I suppose I haven't really been *here*, have I? I'm sorry."

He grabbed her hand over the table, and she squeezed his fingers.

"I appreciate that, but I don't need you around all the time. It would be nice if you and Evvie visited more, though."

"Okay." He squeezed her fingers in return. "We can do that. Have you eaten lunch yet? I can stay for a while."

"Not yet."

Matthias went to the mud room to put on a load of laundry while Loretta made egg salad. She knew Matthias would have preferred ham or turkey for sandwiches, but since he'd been at Evvie's so often, there wasn't any meat in the house anymore.

"So"—Matthias laid out slices of bread for Loretta to put egg salad on them—"you said you were *kind of* working on your website. Care to elaborate?"

Loretta sighed, slopping two large spoonfuls of the mayonnaise-and-egg mixture on the bread. She'd been *kind of* working on it because it frustrated her, so she kept taking fifteen-minute breaks that turned into hour-long breaks.

"Honestly, I'm at a loss about marketing," Loretta said. "What's the point of being able to make a website when you don't know what to put on it or what colors to use or what the most effective calls to action are? I spent most of the morning looking things up, and the more I read, the more I feel like I have no idea what I'm doing."

"Hm." Matthias put their finished sandwiches on plates and took them to the table. "I'm not going to be much help there. We had people to manage that kind of stuff for the band."

"I know. That's fine. I'm not really asking for help—I'm just frustrated." Loretta bit into her sandwich and chewed angrily, not really tasting it. "Tell me why I decided this was a good idea," she said around a mouthful.

Matthias got up and poured them each a glass of water. "It's a good idea because it's something you want to do. You're already doing it, Etta. You've got the right permits, you hired Landon and Gerard for construction, you've got landscapers coming in, you have ideas for the rest of it. It'll take time, but you're making progress. Didn't the tour with Joyce the other day go well?"

"Yes." She took her glass from Matthias. "Thanks."

"There you go then. You have professional approval."

"Yeah, yeah, I guess. She likes the goddesses too." Loretta smiled at the memory of Joyce petting Artemis. It had been bizarre, seeing someone dressed as nicely as Joyce crouching to pet a hen. And she'd seemed genuinely enthralled, which filled Loretta with warmth.

"Even more reason to trust her then, hey?"

"Mm-hmm."

They finished their sandwiches in silence, then Matthias put their dishes in the dishwasher. "Want to show me what you've got so far for your website? I might not know much, but maybe I can give you a new insight or something."

Loretta shrugged. "Worth a try."

They ended up browsing a few wedding venue websites, noting what they liked and didn't like about them. Matthias switched his laundry to the dryer, then they put together a tentative color palette for Loretta's website. "You should hire someone to design a logo, too," Matthias said. "I bet Kat would do that for you. They designed the logo for Creekfest."

Matthias and Nick—the lead singer from Iridium Twilight—had sung a song for Evvie at Creekfest, Juniper Creek's New Year's Eve celebration. It had been sweet, and it successfully brought Evvie and Matthias back together. Loretta had bought a T-shirt there with the Creekfest logo on it; she'd forgotten that Kat, Eleanor's grandchild, had designed it.

"Okay." Loretta jotted a note to contact Kat; it wasn't a bad idea. "I'll do that. Thanks."

Matthias folded his laundry while Loretta looked for logo ideas, asking him occasionally for his thoughts. "Well, good luck," he said a few minutes later. "I've got dinner plans with my lady, but maybe we can do dinner here tomorrow?"

She tried not to gag at the phrase *my lady*, but she didn't hide her grimace as she said, "Sounds good."

Matthias stuck his tongue out at her.

She waved as her brother headed out the door, her mind still on logos and color schemes. Her ideas felt less nebulous now, but she wasn't any more confident.

She thought of Joyce's offer to help her, and part of her wanted to accept. But the last thing she needed was for Joyce—overly chipper, professional wedding planner Joyce—to see how much help she truly needed.

CHAPTER EIGHT

JOYCE

86 DAYS UNTIL THE WEDDING

Joyce hadn't expected Loretta to agree to meet with her, Minnie, and Eleanor to work on a vision board for the wedding, but she looked forward to seeing her again. Loretta's mood had lifted when she showed Joyce around the farm, like being on her home turf put her at ease.

They decided to meet at the library just down the street from the Bluebell.

Loretta was already there when Joyce walked in, sitting at a four-person table near the far wall by the windows. She wore a gray cardigan again today—the same one she'd worn to dinner the other night, likely—over a darker gray T-shirt and jeans with a small rip in the knee.

Before heading over to join her, Joyce went to the front desk. Dylan, the head librarian, stood behind it in a blue-and-red plaid shirt and jeans, doing something on the computer.

"Good morning," Joyce said, and Dylan looked up over her glasses.

"Oh, hey," she said. "I've got the goods." She turned around and picked up a stack of magazines, then slid them across the desk to Joyce. "Will these work?"

"Yes, these are perfect! Thank you." Joyce had requested the magazines the day before, always prepared in advance. "And the scissors and such . . . ?"

"Oh yeah. Here." Dylan reached under the counter and pulled out a basket full of scissors and glue sticks. "Will that work?"

"Yes, thanks again." Joyce put the basket on top of the magazine stack and hefted the whole thing into her arms, trying not to drop the blank board wedged between her elbow and her body. She walked over to the table where Loretta sat, and dropped the stack with an *oof*.

Loretta raised her eyebrows. "What's this?"

"This is our task today." Joyce placed the board in the center of the table and put her hands on her hips, surveying it all with a smile. "It's a bit old-fashioned, but I'm hoping it will help."

Minnie's voice came from behind her. "I like old-fashioned." She joined Joyce and Loretta at the table with Eleanor at her side. "I took orders on paper at the shop until last year when Eleanor made me switch over to a computer."

"Psh." Eleanor gave her a playful glare. "You've admitted more than once that the new electronic system is better."

"Doesn't mean I like it," Minnie said.

The two of them sat at the table, Eleanor between Loretta and Minnie, leaving the chair on Loretta's other side for Joyce.

"No electronic system today, though, I'm afraid," Joyce said, gesturing to the magazines. "We're doing an old-fashioned collage! Dylan kindly gave us these old wedding magazines to go through. We can cut out what we like and paste it to the board as a visionary project to help us all get on the same visual page about the wedding."

"Like a Pinterest board," Eleanor said, grabbing a pair of scissors.

"Exactly!" Joyce turned to her and Minnie. "I know you said

you have a better idea of what you want now, but this could help clarify it even more. What d'you think?"

"I think it's a great idea," Eleanor said, pulling over a couple of magazines.

Minnie shrugged. "Worth a try."

Loretta said nothing but grabbed a pair of scissors when Joyce nudged them over to her.

For the next hour or so, the four of them sat and cut out photos that helped create the rustic atmosphere Minnie and Eleanor wanted for their wedding. Joyce pasted each one on the board as they chatted until she held up the completed collage.

"Ta-da! How's this look?"

"It's not quite right," Minnie said, "but it's coming together."

Eleanor grabbed her hand. "Are you feeling better about the wedding now, though?"

Minnie nodded, although Joyce didn't fully believe her. A small wrinkle between Minnie's eyebrows seemed to say she wasn't quite convinced.

"Good." Eleanor leaned over and kissed Minnie's cheek.

Joyce looked at Loretta to see her reaction, and Loretta gave her a halfhearted thumbs-up.

"Alright, I'd say this was a success then." Or a partial success, at least; Joyce made note to keep an eye on Minnie as the planning progressed.

They chatted more and cleaned up the supplies, then Minnie and Eleanor had to head back to work. Loretta stayed sitting at the table, fiddling with her necklace.

Joyce looked at their charmingly cluttered collage, and a surge of pride flowed through her.

"That was a good idea," Loretta said.

Joyce looked at her in surprise.

"I can tell Minnie's nervous about planning the perfect wedding, and I think this helped." The corners of her lips turned up.

Joyce raised her eyebrows. "I hope so." After a few seconds of silence, she added, "How's your business coming?"

Loretta cleared her throat. "Fine."

"Oh? Did you add those photos to the website?" She swept the remaining paper scraps into the recycling bin she'd brought over earlier, then straightened the scissors and glue sticks in the basket.

"Not yet, but I will."

Joyce stacked everything together again, ready to return it to the front desk.

"Here." Loretta took the completed vision board from her, and Joyce nodded her thanks, puzzled at this waif of a woman who barely spoke yet didn't seem in a hurry to leave.

"I was wondering, actually," Joyce started, "if you'd like to join me at the bakery for a drink." Loretta went to say something, likely to turn Joyce down, but Joyce jumped in with, "I could use company now that Eleanor's gone back to work."

She couldn't figure out why Loretta seemed so against accepting her help, and maybe a more subtle approach would lead to success. Plus, if she was honest, she did feel *something* for Loretta—she was an attractive woman.

Loretta bit her lip, the sight making Joyce's stomach dip. "Sure. Let's get drinks."

"Perfect." Joyce clapped.

The bakery was farther down Main Street toward Minnie's flower shop. Joyce had walked along Main Street a few times, browsing the stores. She'd found a couple cute things in the antique shops, and she'd picked up a piece of fudge from Cavity Central that would likely last her another two weeks.

She'd also visited both Minnie and Eleanor at their shops. Even their businesses complemented each other. While Minnie sold mostly flowers, Eleanor focused on greenery and plant pots. If they wanted to, they could have easily combined their stores. But when Joyce had broached the topic, Minnie's hackles had gone up and Eleanor had changed the subject. Perhaps over the coming months, Joyce would find out what that was all about.

Loretta was quiet on the walk to the bakery, and Joyce ushered her ahead to get her drink first. The display case at the front boasted the regular bakery fare: cookies, cakes, and donuts. But another section of treats had unfamiliar names, possibly Indian. Loretta ordered coffee and a cookie from a woman wearing a lilac hijab whose nametag read "Aaliyah.".

"And for you?" Aaliyah asked Joyce.

Joyce had always been a creature of habit, getting the same meal at every restaurant no matter how good the other menu items sounded. They didn't have her regular café treat here—a Bakewell tart—but they did have a cherry one, so she ordered that and a good old-fashioned English breakfast tea.

Once they had their drinks and treats, they sat at a two-person table by the front window. Joyce crossed one leg over the other. Her black slacks had gotten slightly dusty on the walk over, but she couldn't do much about that. "There we go, then. So, tell me about what you're currently working on for your business." She stirred her tea bag around in her mug, waiting for the tea to darken, and kept her eyes averted to give Loretta space.

Loretta tried to shift her chair, but she'd already backed herself into the corner. The only place she could go was through the window. "Um. Well, I was thinking that making a vision board could be good. Like what we did today."

"Vision boards are always a good idea," Joyce said, trying not to let her excitement show too much, lest she scare Loretta off. "What kinds of things do you have left to work on?"

Loretta rubbed the back of her neck. "The website, the business name, business cards, some kind of system to run it . . ." She clutched her necklace, looking down rather than at Joyce. "I know how to achieve the mechanical side of things—the construction, the landscaping, all of that. But the business side . . ." When she finally raised her gaze, her eyes were wide, her expression almost panicked.

Joyce sat quietly for a moment, contemplating. "Let me help you."

When Loretta shook her head, Joyce reached out and put a hand on her forearm. She went still, her eyes on Joyce's fingers.

"Don't say no yet," Joyce said firmly. "I *want* to help. You'd be doing me a favor by giving me something else to work on while I'm here."

Loretta visibly deflated, as if she couldn't keep up her walls anymore. "I suppose it wouldn't hurt to have your input."

"Thank you." Joyce took the tea bag from her cup and sipped her drink. "How do you feel about learning on the job? You could shadow me while I work on Minnie and Eleanor's wedding. We'll need to work together at times anyway."

Nodding slowly, Loretta said, "That could help me understand my clients better."

"Mm-hmm." Finally, Loretta was coming around. The buzz of victory zipped through Joyce's veins.

"Can I help you any way in return? Besides giving you something else to do?" Loretta asked.

Joyce hadn't expected anything else, but she suspected Loretta needed to feel like they had an even exchange. "If it's not too much trouble, I'll likely need a ride every now and again. We can carpool." She flicked her gaze to Loretta's face, to that wild hair she admired.

"That's reasonable." Loretta sat up straighter and even seemed to breathe easier.

"Good. Then it's settled." They sipped their drinks together in silence for a minute before Joyce got uncomfortable and blurted, "Do you mind if I ask you something?" Her curiosity would nag at her until she knew the answer.

Loretta waved a hand. "Go for it."

"This probably isn't any of my business"—she knew it wasn't, but she could never resist a bit of nosiness—"but you implied you lack experience with weddings. I'm assuming you've never been married yourself?" There, she'd said it.

"Ah." Loretta sipped her coffee. "No, I haven't been." Subtext practically dripped off her words, and Joyce wanted to latch on to it and pull it to the surface.

Andrew and Will would scold her for pushing, but she couldn't help herself. "Did you never want to marry, or . . . ?"

Loretta's jaw clenched. For a moment, Joyce regretted asking. "I did want to get married, when I was younger," Loretta said. "But it didn't work out."

"Oh. I see." Joyce rubbed the back of her neck, wishing she'd kept her mouth shut. Clearly, whatever had happened in Loretta's past had hurt her, and Joyce didn't want to dig it up again.

"What about you?"

"Hm?"

"Were you ever married?" Loretta's gaze flicked to Joyce's left ring finger, empty of a ring.

Joyce laughed. "No. Ironic, isn't it? For a wedding planner to be unmarried?"

"Maybe. Maybe not. Did you never want to marry?"

Joyce supposed she deserved that question, although there was no malice in Loretta's voice. "My situation is rather . . . unique." Explaining her family and romantic situation always posed a challenge. At least with Loretta, it'd be easier since Joyce knew she had no problems with queer people. At some point, Eleanor had mentioned that Loretta was also lesbian. "I live with Will and Andrew, my two best mates. The two of them are together and have been since their twenties. I'm a lesbian, but I always wanted a child, and Will and Andrew wanted a child as well. So, we adopted Tori and raised her together. She explained to me a couple years ago that what we have is called a *queerplatonic relationship*." Her throat thickened on those last words, and she coughed back the urge to cry. Their relationship would be changing in the near future, once she talked to Will and Andrew about Italy. "They're all I've needed. That's the short version."

The long version involved explaining Joyce's messy history with relationships. How when she was stressed, she often latched on to a person and lost herself in a whirlwind of love or lust until she felt sated. How she'd never felt strongly enough for anyone to keep them in her life, to add them to her found family. How she'd never truly *wanted* to add anyone to her family—she liked things how they were.

Loretta looked somewhat stunned. "Wow."

"I bet that's not what you expected when you asked." Joyce laughed again, although it sounded forced.

"Not really, but thank you for telling me." Loretta kept her gaze on Joyce, something akin to admiration in her eyes.

Joyce looked away first, her cheeks burning. "Well, you asked." She tried to keep her voice light, airy, as if she hadn't a care in the world. "That's enough about my personal life. When shall we start working on your business?"

"Do you have plans tomorrow? I can meet you somewhere in town if you want, or at the inn."

"How do you feel about dress shopping? We need to get that done right away since the wedding is soon, so we've planned to look at dresses tomorrow. Evvie, Dylan, Vera, and Kat are coming."

Loretta sat up straighter, her eyes sparkling. "I'd love to come. Are they going for traditional wedding dresses?"

That had been another conflict point for Minnie and Eleanor, and even with the progress they'd made on the vision board that morning, the dress issue hadn't been discussed. Minnie didn't want the fuss of a wedding dress, but Eleanor had convinced her that at least trying on dresses would be fun. "Maybe. We'll see how they feel about it tomorrow once they've tried on a few. It doesn't hurt to look, though, right?"

"Right."

"Perfect. That will be in the afternoon, so we could work on your business in the morning for a bit if you don't mind picking me up. I'd love to see the hens again."

A grin spread across Loretta's face. The love she had for her girls warmed Joyce's heart. "I'm happy to pick you up."

"Alright. Then tomorrow it is."

Joyce's thoughts bounced from topic to topic for the rest of that day: the wedding, her family, Loretta, the hens, and Joyce's own fraught relationship with love and dating. Thoughts of her family hurt the most.

She couldn't sleep that night, so she finally caved and video called Will and Andrew since they'd be awake in Scotland. She'd called them once already with Eleanor and Minnie to say hello, but she hadn't talked to them since.

They caught each other up briefly, then Joyce jumped into it. No point in drawing out the pain. "I've been thinking about Italy," she said.

Will sat up straighter, and Andrew tilted his head in a good imitation of a curious dog. "You have? What have you been thinking?"

She had been thinking about potentially moving to Italy. But as lovely as it sounded, leaving her daughter was akin to cutting out her heart. Will and Andrew were her best friends—more than that, really—but they couldn't expect her to leave Tori, especially after the accident.

The non-choice hurt.

It took her a few seconds to get the words out. "I want you two to go, but I can't. I want to stay with Tori." As soon as she said her daughter's name, the tears started to fall.

Then Will was crying, so she started crying harder, and Andrew had to pull them all together. Not a single tear graced his face, although his voice sounded slightly gruffer than usual, and his bushy eyebrows knit together.

"It's alright," he said. He cleared his throat then continued, "We don't have concrete plans yet. We have time to think about this more."

"And even if we move, you'll always be welcome to visit," Will said, sniffling.

"Of course. I love you both." Joyce rubbed her eyes. She'd broken up with many women in her day, but this felt like the worst of all breakups, and it wasn't even a breakup in the traditional sense of the word.

"We love you too," Will said. "I want to reach through this camera and squeeze you to death."

Joyce laughed through her tears, and the rest of the call felt lighter. Her sadness returned, though, after she'd hung up.

Her meeting with Loretta the following day fell next on her agenda, so that's where she tried to direct her thoughts. She fell asleep thinking about Loretta, her hens, and her charming farm. Those thoughts didn't hurt at all.

CHAPTER NINE

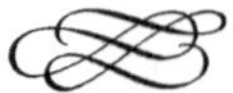

LORETTA

*L*oretta waited in the car for Joyce the next morning, having texted that she'd arrived at the Bluebell. Joyce came out with her briefcase and wedding board, looking as business-y as usual in gray slacks and a pink flowy blouse, her hair in a neat bun at the base of her head.

"Good morning," Joyce said cheerily as she slid into the passenger seat, bringing a faint scent of orange blossoms with her. "How are you today?"

"I'm well, thank you. And you?"

"I'm alright. I didn't have the best sleep, but on the bright side, I just had a call with Tori."

Loretta glanced at her, and the tightness around Joyce's mouth contrasted with the cheer in her voice. "Oh? And how is she?"

Loretta couldn't scrutinize Joyce's expression as she drove, so she settled on listening for any note of strain in Joyce's voice.

"She seems to be managing fine without me. She takes people on wildlife tours off the coast in Banff, where we live. Our boat is

"

called the *Guillemot Guide*. Will used to be skipper on it, but . . . well, he's retiring soon." Her voice shook slightly on those last words.

"Huh." Loretta knew about the boat, but she hadn't expected Joyce's family to have ties to nature. "Does Tori give tours often?"

"Yes, quite often. The largest mainland gannet colony is near us, and it's a more popular tourist attraction than you'd think." The more Joyce spoke, the less Loretta could tell if something was bothering her. That tremor in her voice was the only indication that something was off.

"Oh, so that's why you like my girls. You've got experience with birds!"

Joyce laughed. "I've never interacted with gannets up close, and I don't think I'd like to. Did you know they have the largest wingspan of any seabird in the northern hemisphere?"

"I didn't," Loretta said, impressed even though she couldn't picture a gannet in her head. She couldn't picture Joyce on a boat, either—it seemed too wild for her.

"We see plenty of other birds on the tours too, of course: guillemots, kittiwakes, puffins, cormorants. All kinds of sea birds."

"Puffins? I've always wanted to see one but never got the chance." They looked like miniature blushing penguins with large beaks, and Loretta wanted to scoop them up and carry them around like she did with her hens.

"Maybe you'll have to visit me one day to see them," Joyce said. The comment may have been lighthearted, but Loretta's heartbeat sped up the tiniest bit at the idea of watching seabirds with Joyce.

"Maybe. Do you see any marine animals?"

They talked about the wildlife tours and the sea life off the northeast coast of Scotland until they arrived at the farm. Loretta hadn't heard Joyce talk about herself this much before, and she wanted to know more. From what Loretta gathered, Joyce lived in a town even smaller than Juniper Creek. They launched their tours from a dock across a bridge in a town called Macduff, and spring was their most lucrative season.

"It's mating season," Joyce said. "Seabirds spend most of their lives at sea, obviously, so if you want to watch them for an extended period of time, you have to plan your trip for when they're on land." Loretta made a mental note to look up Scottish seabirds later; they sounded fascinating.

Once they settled at Loretta's kitchen table with cups of coffee, Joyce asked, "So, what can I help you with today? You mentioned a website, right? We could start there."

"Sure. I've been working on a few things, and I'd like your thoughts." Loretta pulled up the color palette she'd started, along with the draft website and her logo ideas.

As Joyce gave her feedback—in a surprisingly gentle way—Loretta grew more excited about her business. Marketing didn't seem nearly as scary when she had someone to walk her through it. She wondered if the whole thing had even been that hard in the first place, or if the amount of information had simply over-whelmed her to the point that she couldn't break it into manage-able steps.

"Just get something up there," Joyce said. "Your website doesn't have to be perfect, and having something up is better than having nothing. You can refine it later. Here, I made a list for you." She neatly ripped a page out of her notebook, which had a checklist labeled "Loretta's Business To-Dos" at the top. "The starred ones are essentials and should be done first, and the ones highlighted in green are optional."

For some inexplicable reason, Joyce's organizational skills flooded Loretta's lower stomach with warmth. She'd never expected someone *being organized* would turn her on, and yet here she was.

"I can't help with whatever this is, though." Joyce waved at the coding on Loretta's screen. "That's all nonsense to me."

"I've got that part covered." Loretta shifted in her seat, her cheeks heating.

"You can code?"

"I can. Would you like another cup?" Loretta grabbed Joyce's empty mug and took it with hers to the counter, glad for the chance to turn around and hide her face.

"Yes, please. Tea this time, though, if that's alright. How'd you learn to do that?"

"Put on the kettle?" Loretta glanced over her shoulder and caught Joyce scowling good-naturedly. She smirked. "I worked in tech in California for a while, developing a few of the earlier computers." She paused and huffed out a laugh. "Damn, that makes me sound old."

"No older than I am," Joyce said wryly. "I'm impressed. Coding seems difficult, and I've always admired people who can work on the back end of tech things."

Loretta paused before picking up the kettle. She'd never really seen her coding skills as impressive before. "It's not that hard, once you know what you're doing."

Joyce scoffed. "Don't be modest. I'm sure it's more difficult than you think. You're simply used to it."

"Maybe." Loretta poured water for them both, leaving Joyce's teabag in her mug. She'd noticed at the bakery that Joyce liked her tea strong. "How'd you get into wedding planning?"

Joyce's expression took on a dreamy quality, her face softening and her gaze drifting into the distance as she remembered some-thing Loretta couldn't see. "I wanted to plan weddings since I was ten years old because of my aunt."

Loretta placed the steaming cup in front of her, then sat next to her. "Was she a wedding planner?"

"No, she was a waitress." Joyce refocused on Loretta. "You need context here. I have seven siblings, and my parents didn't really have time for all of us. They had clear favorites too, and I wasn't one of them."

Seven siblings? Loretta had struggled enough with *one*, although she and Matthias had become close later in life.

Joyce continued, "My aunt had singled me out for some

reason, though. Possibly, she saw something of herself in me. But she seemed to be the only adult who cared. She used to bring me books and take me to the park. She taught me about flowers and told me all about the new fashions—things I found interesting at that age that no one else talked about with me. Anyway, she was getting married, and she asked if I'd like to be the flower girl. I said yes, of course." Her face took on that faraway look again. "I know brides are the star of the show, but back then, in my flower girl dress with everyone's eyes on me, I thought *I* was the center of attention. I got ready with my aunt and her bridesmaids, I walked down the aisle all by myself, and I even got to hold a bouquet. In my ten-year-old mind, that was magic."

The expression of bliss on Joyce's face lingered as she looked back at Loretta, her blue eyes shining like drops of the ocean. Loretta believed wholeheartedly that people became their best selves when they spoke about what they loved. Joyce's best self glowed, lighting her up from the inside.

"Weddings *are* magic," Loretta said. "That's why I want to be part of them. I want to create that magic for other people." She could still feel that sense of longing in her chest when she pictured the two people standing on the church steps two years ago, so sure of each other.

"And you will." Joyce put her hand on Loretta's arm, her fingernails painted blush pink. Loretta fought the urge to shiver at that slight touch, tingles bursting on her skin where Joyce's fingers lay. "I fully believe this place will set an enchanting scene for Eleanor and Minnie and many clients after them."

Loretta tried to let Joyce's praise wash over her instead of shrinking under the weight of it. "Speaking of enchanting, there is one thing I forgot to mention the other day that I'd love help with." Joyce had proven her ability to help without judgment, and Loretta wanted her opinion.

They put their shoes and jackets on, and Joyce followed Loretta outside. They stopped by the chicken enclosure so Joyce could say hi to the girls, then they went to the barn. Once they stood inside, the space still dim and lifeless before them, Loretta gestured to the dangling wires. "I don't know if you remember from my sketches, but I envision chandeliers in here. Something to elevate the space and bring in that sense of enchantment. I think market lights would work as well, but don't you think a central light fixture would tie it all together?"

Joyce crossed her arms, tapping her foot lightly on the wooden floor as she stared at the ceiling. "I see what you mean. Have you looked online?"

"I have, but it's difficult to imagine what something truly looks like when all you see is a product photo. And I don't want something you can get just anywhere. I want this space to be unique." Loretta realized that could sound snobby, but she wanted what she wanted.

"Hmm."

"I looked at the antique stores in town, but nothing in them would work."

Joyce's eyes widened in horror. "Oh god, did you see that monstrosity in Mabel's Antiques?"

"You saw it too?" Loretta laughed. "It was horrible!"

"Who needs hundreds of crystal penises hanging above their heads? No one." Joyce shuddered, making Loretta laugh even harder.

"We'll need to look for decor for the wedding anyway, so why don't we put *shopping for light fixtures* on our to-do list? There are towns nearby we can look in, right? And Vancouver isn't that far, from what I understand."

"That works." Joyce was proving fun to spend time with, and Loretta was grudgingly grateful for her help.

The sound of a growling stomach interrupted their conversation, and Joyce put a hand on her abdomen, looking sheepish. "How do you feel about getting lunch before we pick up the others?"

The group of dress shoppers had decided to split into two cars and look at dresses separately so Minnie and Eleanor wouldn't see each other's dresses before the wedding day. Joyce had explained it was more about the *big reveal* moment than a superstition about bad luck.

"That's a good idea. We can go to the diner, if that works with you."

Joyce agreed, and the two of them went inside to gather their things.

Now that Loretta had a better idea of how to set up her business online, and now that Joyce had offered to help find the perfect light fixtures, excitement bubbled up in her like it had when she'd first come up with the venue idea. They had a plan, and they'd already put it in motion.

She didn't have to flounder any longer, not with Joyce around.

CHAPTER TEN

JOYCE

*J*oyce enjoyed helping Loretta with her business. It brought her back to the days of building her client base and figuring out how to optimize her branding. She'd consulted for a few other wedding planners over the years as well, and it brought new life to her creativity every time. Helping Loretta was no exception.

Loretta seemed enthusiastic and engaged the entire morning, so unlike how she'd been when she'd first met Joyce. She even laughed multiple times, the sound of it unexpectedly rich and musical. Joyce could listen to her laugh all day.

Her positivity continued over lunch as they talked more about the wedding.

The day looked bright until they picked up Minnie and Kat. Minnie's expression was pinched as she followed Kat out to the car.

"Ready to go?" Joyce asked, infusing her voice with brightness. Some brides couldn't wait to try on dresses, but others dreaded the experience. Both reactions had merit; shopping for a wedding dress could be fun, but it could also lead to tears and self-loathing spirals. Joyce did everything in her power to avoid the latter.

"Let's get this over with," Minnie said as she buckled her seatbelt.

So, she was dreading it. Joyce prepared herself to play the consoling friend and the hype woman, possibly also the mediator between Minnie and the dress consultant. She glanced at Kat, raising an eyebrow and tilting her head slightly toward Minnie.

Kat grimaced and ran a hand through their short red hair.

Right. Joyce needed to start building the hype as soon as she could. And Loretta could help. "Loretta, do you mind if we put on music? Minnie, what do you like to listen to?"

Minnie shrugged, but Kat pulled out their phone. "I have a playlist, if that's okay."

It took a minute for Loretta to connect Kat's phone to the speakers, then "Unchained Melody" by the Righteous Brothers began to play.

Minnie's lips twitched, and she nudged Kat. "How did you know I like this song?"

"I know you." They shot Minnie a smile. "Plus, Gran says this song reminds her of you."

"She does?" Minnie's cheeks turned pink, and Joyce turned to face forward again, satisfied. Kat knew what they were doing.

Loretta glanced at Joyce and blew out a small sigh. She must have noticed Minnie's mood as well.

When Joyce had asked earlier about why Kat decided to help Minnie rather than their grandmother, Eleanor had said, "I have a good idea of what I want already. Minnie, on the other hand . . . She needs the support more than I do."

Now, with Minnie in the car wearing a pained expression, Joyce saw what Eleanor meant. But maybe everything would go better than expected after Minnie tried on a few dresses.

Minutes later, once they'd parked and entered the shop in Chilliwack, Joyce reconsidered. Minnie looked even more miserable now than she had in the car, her arms crossed tightly across her body, her jaw tense. She focused more on the ground than on any of the dresses hanging on the racks around them.

"Are you alright?" Joyce asked. "We don't have to do this if you don't want to."

Minnie shook her head. "We're here. Let's look."

Joyce pressed her lips together and followed the dress consultant to another row.

"Do you know what type of dress you'd like?" the consultant, a short woman with a blond bob, asked Minnie.

Minnie cringed. "Not really."

"That's not a problem," the consultant said. "We can try a few different styles. Since your wedding is coming up soon, that does limit our options. But I'm sure we can find the perfect dress, and we can always alter it for you. How about this one?"

She gestured to a glossy ballgown dress with a pleated tulle skirt.

When Minnie didn't respond, Joyce said, "That might be too much. Let's try something plainer, more demure. How does that sound?"

"Okay." Minnie's shoulders eased slightly. From behind her, Kat gave Joyce a thumbs-up.

Loretta had been trailing at the back of the group, but she moved to the front as they looked at more dresses, pointing out things Minnie might like. Even if she didn't know Minnie well, she clearly cared enough about her to try and lighten the atmosphere.

The consultant pulled a few more dresses, then Loretta, Kat, and Joyce sat in the fitting room while Minnie went to change into the first dress. Kat called Minnie's best friend, Dot, on their phone, pulling her up on video. Dot lived in Calgary and couldn't fly out for dress shopping, but she wanted to be involved.

"How's she doing?" Dot asked, her tone concerned.

With Minnie out of the room, Joyce could talk freely.

"She seems quite uncomfortable. Is she alright?" she asked Kat.

Kat shook their head. "Honestly, I don't think she wants a dress. I think she's doing this for Gran."

Loretta frowned. "When you say *this*, do you mean the wedding or getting a dress?"

"The dress. She wants a wedding, although she's been clashing a bit with Gran on that topic too. Gran wants something big and fun, but that's not really Minnie's style. I suggested a suit for her, but she brushed me off. I'm kind of worried about her."

"I know the feeling," Dot said from Kat's phone. "She's been putting on a brave face, but I can tell she's stressed about the whole thing."

Kat's and Dot's words confirmed Joyce's suspicions. Minnie and Eleanor hadn't expressed their disagreements in so many words, but Joyce figured their concepts of the ideal wedding differed. She'd seen a hint of it at the first planning dinner then again during their collage session.

"She shouldn't get a dress if she doesn't want a dress," Loretta said firmly.

"I agree wholeheartedly," Joyce said as Kat nodded and Dot made an affirmative noise. "Let's see what she thinks when she comes back in."

The expression on Minnie's face said it all as she walked in wearing an A-line dress with a lace bodice. Her face was carefully blank, her jaw still tight, and she walked stiffly, as if she didn't know how to move with this much fabric on.

"Go ahead and stand up there." The consultant gestured to the small pedestal in front of a three-way mirror. "See what you think." She helped Minnie onto the pedestal.

Minnie looked at herself and swallowed hard. "Not this one," she said.

"Hey, Min," Dot said gently from Kat's phone, "are you sure you want a dress?"

Minnie blinked quickly, and Joyce had a feeling she was blinking back tears. "I want to try on another one."

She followed the consultant back to the fitting room.

"She looks like she's being tortured," Loretta said. "We've got to get her out of this. It's clearly not what she wants."

"Good luck," Kat said with a sigh. "When Minnie decides she's doing something, it's like herding cats to change her mind."

Dot groaned in frustration and adjusted her headwrap. "If only I could be there right now, I'd knock some sense into her. And give her a hug."

"I haven't herded cats, but I can herd chickens." Loretta scooched closer to Joyce. "Have you been in this scenario before?"

Joyce nodded. "Unfortunately, yes. Sometimes a client needs tough love, especially if they won't admit what they really want."

"We can do that, if we have to," Loretta said, sitting up straight on the edge of the couch. She seemed determined to put up a united front with Joyce, and Joyce couldn't help but smile.

They would get Minnie through this, together.

When Minnie returned, she wore a silk chiffon draped gown that suited her much better than the last dress. She didn't look as awkward in it, but she still wasn't smiling.

"What do you think?" Minnie asked, stepping onto the pedestal.

"What do *you* think?" Dot parroted.

Minnie turned slightly left and right, examining herself from different angles. "This isn't . . . me," she said. "It's not bad, but . . ."

"But you don't like it," Loretta said, and Minnie nodded.

"Do you mind if we talk to her for a minute?" Joyce asked the consultant. "Alone?"

"Of course." As soon as the consultant left, Joyce and Loretta got up and crossed over to Minnie, one on either side of her. Kat held their phone so Dot could see.

"Do you wear dresses in your daily life?" Joyce kept her voice soft.

Minnie shook her head. "I have before, but I don't anymore."

"And why is that?"

Minnie flicked her gaze to Loretta, then to Kat, then up at the ceiling. "They make me uncomfortable. I don't feel like myself in them." At least Minnie had admitted that much.

"And you never have, Min," Dot added. "Even when we were younger."

"Why wear a dress for your wedding, then?" Joyce asked.

Minnie opened her mouth to answer, then burst into tears.

"Oh, bollocks," Joyce said under her breath. This was not what she'd meant to happen.

Kat sprang to their feet and rushed over. "Hey, it's okay," they said, helping Minnie off the pedestal and to the couch where Kat's phone sat, Dot protesting at being left out of the loop.

Minnie sat with Kat beside her, their arm around her shoulders.

Loretta knelt in front of Minnie. "Deep breaths," she said, holding Minnie's hands in hers. "I want you to breathe with me, okay? I'm going to count. In, two, three, four . . . out, two, three, four . . ."

Joyce had gotten the impression at first that Loretta wasn't great with people. But she was starting to see what Loretta hid under the surface, a glimmer of a compassionate heart shining through her seemingly grouchy exterior.

After a few breathing cycles, Minnie had calmed down enough to talk. Loretta pulled a tissue out of her purse and gave it to Minnie, who held it to her nose. "I just," she said, sniffling, "want this wedding to be perfect for Eleanor. And she loves dresses. Classic, beautiful wedding dresses."

Kat squeezed her shoulder. "She does. But she likes them for *her*, not for you. Not if that's not what *you* want."

"I don't know Eleanor well," Loretta said, patting Minnie's knee, "but I have a feeling she'll love whatever you wear because you'll be the one wearing it."

Joyce's heart swelled at her advice—the perfect words to comfort a torn bride. Why hadn't she thought to say that earlier? Loretta had been worried she didn't know much about the wedding business, but she had the right instincts for it.

Minnie sniffed but nodded reluctantly. "I suppose."

An idea arose in Joyce's mind—something Minnie could wear

that she'd feel comfortable in. Something that wasn't a dress. "You all stay here," she said. "I'll be right back."

She found the consultant at a nearby rack and explained the situation. When she made her request, the consultant's eyes lit up and she told Joyce to follow her.

Ten minutes later, Joyce found Minnie still sitting on the couch, talking to Dot, Kat, and Loretta. "I have something you might like," Joyce said, holding a hand out to Minnie. "It's not a dress."

Minnie's forehead smoothed in relief then creased again as she frowned in confusion. "Is it a suit? I'm not sure I want to wear a suit either."

"It's not a suit. Come with me."

With her eyes narrowed, Minnie put her hand in Joyce's and let Joyce lead her to the change room. "How do you feel about this?" Joyce said, holding up an ivory jumpsuit.

"I'd have to see it on," Minnie replied, tilting her head.

Fair enough. Joyce helped Minnie into the jumpsuit. As soon as she zipped up the garment, Minnie wiggled around and bent both knees a few times. "This is comfortable," she said, sounding surprised.

"Let's see how it looks." Joyce walked out front with her again, and the expressions on everyone's faces were a good sign. No one frowned. No one grimaced. Loretta even raised her eyebrows in a way that said *I'm impressed*, and Dot let out a quiet "Wow."

Minnie stepped onto the pedestal once again, and a slow smile grew on her face as she looked at herself. The jumpsuit had short lace sleeves and a modest V-cut neckline. Lace cuffs around the hems of the pantlegs matched the sleeves, but the rest of the suit lacked any adornment.

Minnie turned side to side, posing a few different ways. "Oh, it has pockets!" She stuck her hands into said pockets, laughing. Her eyes glittered, this time not with tears.

"What do you think?" Joyce asked.

Minnie grinned at her. "I think you're good at your job. And I think I quite like this . . . what did you call it? A jumpsuit?" She turned around. "What does my audience say?"

"Oh, Min, that is so *you*," Dot said, her hand over her smile.

Kat nodded, their eyes bright. "I love it."

"It suits you." Loretta smiled at Minnie, then at Joyce, and something glinted in her eyes. A dash of pride, maybe? "If you're happy with it, then it's perfect."

Minnie looked at herself once more and giggled. "I am happy with it, and I think Eleanor will be too."

"She will," Kat agreed.

Joyce tried not to preen as she helped Minnie out of the jumpsuit. They'd somehow avoided disaster—all of them, working as a team. And Loretta had proved she could handle complications. If Joyce hadn't had full confidence in her before, she sure did now.

She admired Loretta. The way she'd soothed Minnie, the way she'd insisted Minnie not wear a dress if she didn't want to, the way she'd looked at Joyce as if she admired Joyce too, in some way . . . Joyce couldn't wait to work on the rest of the wedding with her.

CHAPTER ELEVEN

LORETTA

Dress shopping hadn't gone how Loretta had expected, but the important thing was that Minnie had an outfit she felt happy and comfortable in. Joyce had thought fast on her feet with the jumpsuit idea, and Loretta couldn't help but be impressed at her decisiveness and surety. Watching Joyce in action —figuring out not only what Minnie wanted but what she *needed* —made Loretta like her even more.

On the ride home, Minnie called Eleanor to share her news about their successful shopping trip, and she shouted that Eleanor had found her dress. No matter how much Minnie tried to wheedle details out of Eleanor, she wouldn't give any. The call ended when Kat wrestled the phone away from Minnie, the two of them laughing in the back seat.

Joyce and Loretta looked at each other, smiles taking over both their faces, and something passed between them, Loretta was sure of it. She didn't know what it was. Camaraderie, maybe? A shared feeling of satisfaction? Whatever it was, Loretta found herself looking forward to working with Joyce more, despite how she could be pushy at times.

The giddiness running through her veins faded once she got home, but she carried her happiness with her as she grabbed her sketchbook and went out back to sit with the girls. Rain pattered around her, but the chicken enclosure had a cover, so she didn't worry about getting wet. Her paper became damp in the humidity, but she'd dealt with that before.

She focused on Athena, who pecked around her feet. As Athena's feathers took shape under her pencil, her mind drifted to earlier that day as she worked with Joyce on her business.

Loretta's chest filled with warmth as she remembered how Joyce had taken an interest in her coding skills, how she'd been eager to see the chickens, how she suggested they look for light fixtures together.

The back door of the house opened, startling Loretta out of her reverie.

"Sorry," Matthias said. "I guess I could have knocked, but it feels weird to knock when you're *leaving* the house instead of entering."

"It's fine," Loretta said, her hand over her heart. "I just lost two years of life, that's all."

Matthias rolled his eyes. "Did you forget we were coming over for dinner?"

"Me? Forget? Never." She had definitely forgotten, her mind occupied by the events of the day. "Was I supposed to cook something . . . ?"

Matthias guffawed. "Wow, you did forget. Is something going on with you? You're usually on top of things like this."

Loretta shook her head. "Just thinking about dress shopping. Minnie got a jumpsuit!"

"I don't know what that is, but cool. Don't tell Evvie, though, otherwise she'll have to keep it secret from Eleanor, and you know how she feels about secrets."

"Noted. I'll keep my lips zipped."

She went inside and said hello to Evvie, and the three of them ordered pizza and watched a YA romcom Evvie wanted to see called *Red, White & Royal Blue*. Loretta didn't often watch romcoms, but the movie was cute.

Matthias and Evvie seemed content to snuggle as the credits rolled, so Loretta got up to put on the kettle. She leaned against the counter as the water boiled, and she looked at her brother and his girlfriend, their heads close together, their voices a low murmur as they talked. Loretta had the urge to grab her sketchbook and capture the moment on paper.

She wanted their love to last.

A tug under her breastbone made her frown. Was she jealous of her brother? She'd had this feeling a few times over the past few weeks, usually when she was around another couple. But that was ridiculous. She had no interest in finding romance again—it would never work out for her.

Joyce's shining smile flitted through her thoughts, and she frowned at herself, tugging on her Magen David necklace. She felt pleasantly unsteady around Joyce, and she hadn't felt that way since Gail.

But that didn't mean she was looking for romance again. Not with Joyce, not with anyone. After what happened with Gail, she couldn't take another heartbreak.

LORETTA TOOK the next few days to recover from all the socializing. While she enjoyed being out and about again—especially with Joyce there to help with her business—her social batteries needed recharging. Plus, taking time away from people would help her clear her head. She'd had romance on the brain an odd amount lately, likely because of the wedding.

Withdrawing to her introverted happy place, Loretta slept, read a book about eels, sketched, and picked up one of her embroidery projects she'd abandoned a few months ago.

On Wednesday, while she sat outside with the girls, Gerard walked up to the enclosure and cleared his throat. He and Landon had been hard at work on the barn, as usual, fixing the loft.

"Sorry to interrupt," he said. He wore his construction

uniform: worn brown Carhartt overalls, a long-sleeved black shirt, and boots. He stuck one hand in his pocket, the other holding a gray hard hat.

Loretta closed her sketchbook. "Oh, not at all. What's up?"

"We've finished with the loft. Would you like to look every-thing over?" He smoothed his thick, dark mustache as he waited for her answer.

"Um, sure. Lead the way." Loretta had no idea what to look for. She didn't really know what needed fixing in the first place, besides the obviously rotten boards. But it seemed like Gerard wanted her approval, so she'd give it.

The smell of freshly cut wood hit her nose as she entered the barn, and she breathed in deeply. She'd always loved that smell; it made her think of her father and his endless woodworking projects. He hadn't had much time for them, but he'd made time when he could.

Gerard clomped up the stairs to the loft and Loretta followed.

Landon stood inside the space, arms crossed as he looked around. His outfit mirrored his father's, and Loretta imagined he resembled a younger Gerard, before the mustache had grown in. "Hey Loretta," he said. "Come to check our work?"

"As much as I can. I have no doubt you've both done a wonderful job."

From what she could tell, they had. Fewer holes pierced the walls, and there were new sturdy boards in place of the old rotting ones. They'd also replaced an entire section of the gabled roof. "It looks perfect," she said.

Gerard grunted, which Loretta took as affirmation.

"Awesome. I'm going to miss working here," Landon said.

Loretta turned to look at him, his dark skin glowing in the warm afternoon light filtering in from outside. "You are?"

"Yeah. It's nice to get out of town, closer to nature. And this barn has character, you know? It's gonna be a great space for weddings." Pride radiated in his voice and his stature as he looked around once more. "Thanks for hiring us."

Tears pressed unexpectedly at the backs of her eyes at Landon's words. Every time someone else saw her vision, it surprised her and made her feel like maybe she could actually accomplish something. "Of course. This place wouldn't be the same without you."

She'd already paid them, so they said their goodbyes and went on their way. Loretta went downstairs to the barn's main floor and stood in the middle, visualizing where everything would go. Only a couple of months until the first wedding. Life would fill this place, laughter echoing off the walls, feet scuffing the floor as people danced.

Only a few things remained to finish, two of them being the light fixtures and the paint. She could have hired someone to paint the barn for her—in fact, she *had* hired someone to paint the outside—but she wanted a role in the renovating as well. She'd painted walls before, so she figured she could do the inside, her creaky bones be damned. She'd leave the loft its rustic brown, but the main floor would be white.

The walls seemed so large, though. How long would it take her to paint this entire place by herself? With the wedding approaching quickly and so much left to do, she needed help.

She wanted Joyce's opinion on paint colors anyway, so why not ask Joyce? Loretta tried to imagine Joyce painting walls and laughed. She'd have to wear a poncho to protect her business outfits, so prim and proper.

But it didn't hurt to ask.

CHAPTER TWELVE

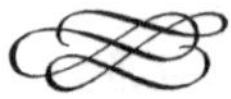

JOYCE

78 DAYS UNTIL THE WEDDING

Joyce sat on a stool at the back counter of Thistles and Stems, doing her best to repot a few plants into the quirky pots Eleanor had given her. An apron protected her trousers and blouse, which she was grateful for. She needed to pick up a few more casual clothes, especially since she'd agreed to help Loretta paint the barn on Monday.

"You don't have to do this, you know," Eleanor said, arranging a bouquet for a customer. "I appreciate the help, but I can't pay you."

Joyce waved her off, trying not to fling dirt at her. "I like being useful," she said, patting soil around a succulent she had transplanted into a pastel-blue llama pot. "I don't have much to do, really. You've made wedding planning easy on me."

"Sorry, I can attempt to complicate the wedding, if you'd like," Eleanor said with a wink.

"Tempting, but I'll pass. How are you feeling about things so far?" They'd spoken about specific topics like Eleanor's dress, the venue, and catering, but they hadn't truly talked about the wedding as friends. The ease they used to have with each other had disappeared somewhere in the years they'd been apart, and Joyce grasped at it every time they were together. Their current relationship as client and contractor didn't help.

"About the wedding? I'm feeling quite good." A note of insecurity peeked through those words; Joyce had her fair share of experience listening for it, especially when people spoke about their wedding.

"Are you?" Joyce asked, turning her full attention to her friend.

Eleanor sighed and dropped her hands from the flower arrangement in front of her. "Mostly, yes. I am a tad worried, though. Since we jumped into planning, Minnie has seemed more stressed. I wonder if this is too much for her."

As far as Joyce knew, no one had told Eleanor about Minnie's breakdown regarding the dress. Minnie's anxiety must have overflowed into other areas of her life.

"When we started looking at wedding services," Eleanor said, "Minnie threw up a wall. She didn't want to look at any vendors outside of people she already knew. Eventually she looked with me, but she didn't seem all that interested. More frustrated, I think. So I agreed to work with people we knew. I hoped you could help smooth the process, which you have, but she doesn't seem much less stressed." She pushed her glasses up her nose. "I'm scared she doesn't actually want to get married. But she's the one who proposed, so I'm confused."

Joyce had dealt with confused spouses-to-be more times than she could count.

"Weddings can be tough on people's emotions," she said. "All you can do is talk to her and make sure she's comfortable with everything. I can help as we work on things, but she has to speak up if she's not happy with something. It's not your responsibility to read her mind."

Eleanor pursed her lips thoughtfully. "You're right. I think . . . somewhere in the last couple of months, we lost sight of each other because we've been so focused on the wedding. I'll sit down with her tonight and have a good heart-to-heart. Thank you."

She wrapped an arm around Joyce and squeezed her shoulders.

"Of course."

"How are *you* feeling about everything?" Eleanor asked, sliding eucalyptus leaves in among the flowers of the bouquet. "I know you haven't worked much with Loretta yet, but has it been alright with her shadowing you?"

"Oh, yes. It took a while for her to accept my help, but it's been fine so far." Better than fine, really. "I think we make a good team."

She told Eleanor about their plans to start painting the barn on Monday, and as she spoke, her excitement grew. Not just to work on the barn more, but to get to know Loretta better. Something about her intrigued Joyce, and her thoughts had drifted to Loretta often in the past few days. She wasn't sure what that was all about, but she didn't dwell on it. Instead, she embraced the feeling of warmth and anticipation that washed over her whenever she thought of going to the farm.

Only a few more days to go.

~

75 DAYS UNTIL THE WEDDING

On Monday morning, Joyce woke up early. Jet lag hadn't lasted long, and she'd managed to get back to her normal routine in terms of her sleep schedule. She got ready and ordered an omelet from Dean, then she returned upstairs to work on a new puzzle she'd bought. It barely fit on the desk in her hotel room, but she couldn't go for months without working on a puzzle.

She knew Tori would be awake—Scotland was nine hours ahead of British Columbia—so she called her daughter, propping up the phone so they could see each other and she could work on the puzzle at the same time.

"Hiya, Mum," Tori said when she answered. Her hair brushed her shoulders, free from its bun. "Isn't it early to be calling me?"

"Not for me. I'm going out after lunch anyway, so I thought I'd check in."

"Where're you off to?"

"I'm going to work on the barn today with Loretta, the woman who owns it. Construction is finished, so now we've got to paint it."

"Are you sure you're up for that?"

"What's that supposed to mean?"

"Well . . . you aren't as young as you once were, Mum. I don't want you to hurt your back or something."

Joyce scoffed. "Not you too. Your fathers have been on my case already. If I can walk around in heels all day, I can bloody well paint a wall."

"Of course you can," Tori said, and Joyce rolled her eyes.

"Mm-hmm." Joyce fit another puzzle piece in place. "Aha! I knew I had seen that piece somewhere." She glanced at Tori on her phone screen—her daughter also had a puzzle going. At least they could bond this way while on opposite sides of the world. "Anyway, you should see Loretta's charming little farmhouse. She owns five hens all named after Greek goddesses, and she let me pet them the other day."

"Why Greek goddesses?"

"I don't know, actually. I'll ask her."

"So the barn is nice?"

"Oh, yes. Loretta drew pictures of her vision for it, and it's gorgeous. You'll love it, Tor. You should see Loretta's drawings, too. She's truly an artist."

"Mum?"

"Yes?"

Tori looked into the camera intently. "Are you sure you don't want to go to Italy with Dad and Da?"

Joyce set down the puzzle piece she'd been trying to find a home for, her heart beating harder in her chest. "I thought about it for a while, Tor. I think . . . I don't think I could be truly happy being away from you."

"But what about being away from your best friends?"

She sighed, her throat thick. "It's not going to be easy, no matter how you slice it. But I've made my decision. I'm staying with you."

"Okay." Tori smiled, and her eyes were misty. "I'm glad you won't be leaving."

The warmth that filled Joyce at those words solidified that she'd made the right choice, even if it hurt.

They talked for another half hour or so, then Joyce kept working on her puzzle until she got hungry.

She met Eleanor for lunch at the diner across the street, giving the two of them a chance to catch up more. They'd missed so much time together after Amara had passed away and Eleanor had isolated herself. Sometimes it baffled Joyce that they'd gotten to this point, sitting in a diner in Canada, chatting about Eleanor's second wedding.

Joyce's phone went off, and she smiled when she saw the text.

"Who's that, then?" Eleanor asked.

"Loretta. She's picking me up for our painting afternoon."

"Right. Have fun! I should get back to work anyway. I've overstayed my lunch break."

The two of them walked outside, and Joyce's heart lifted when her eyes landed on Loretta's car. She frowned, puzzled at herself. Surely she shouldn't be this excited to see an acquaintance and coworker.

It had to be the thought of seeing the hens again. That explained it.

CHAPTER THIRTEEN

LORETTA

As soon as Joyce entered the car and the smell of orange blossoms swirled in the air, Loretta's entire body relaxed. Somehow, Joyce acted as a balm to her nerves, sanding down the edges of her anxiety.

"You're wearing overalls," Loretta blurted, then slapped her hand over her mouth. She hadn't meant to comment on Joyce's clothes, but seeing her in something not businesslike surprised her. She pulled onto the main road, glancing at Joyce.

Joyce raised her eyebrows. "I am wearing *dungarees*, yes. Aren't they a good choice of painting outfit?"

"Dungarees?" Loretta let the word roll over her tongue; it was fun to say. "I haven't heard that one before. But yes, they are. I just wasn't sure . . ." She'd backed herself into a corner with this one.

"You weren't sure if I'd show up in paint-appropriate clothing." Joyce rolled her eyes, not unkindly. "What would you have done if I'd worn a skirt and heels?"

"I suppose I would lend you clothes."

Joyce looked her up and down, and blood rushed to Loretta's face. She kept her gaze forward, trying to ignore the pleasure that ran through her at having Joyce look at her like that.

"I'm not sure I'd fit into anything you own," Joyce said.

"You hate my clothes that much, hey?" Loretta kept her voice light as she turned onto the highway.

"Excuse me, I do not. I could rock a pair of jeans and a T-shirt any day."

"You could. And I'm sure you'd look great in them." Just like how she looked great in those overalls.

Loretta looked at Joyce, expecting a reply—hoping for some gesture to tell her she hadn't stepped out of line—but Joyce stared at her with her mouth parted, a slightly stunned expression on her face.

"Anyway," Loretta said, not keen to let the silence last, "I already picked up the paint, but we have to prime everything first. There's no way we can get the whole thing done in a day."

Joyce snorted, Loretta's previous comment seemingly forgotten. "Not unless you've got amphetamines in your purse."

"I don't, unfortunately. My dealer was all out. You can check if you don't believe me."

"You need to get a better dealer then," Joyce said, and Loretta shot her a wide grin.

They kept the conversation light until they arrived at the farm. Loretta had set up the painting supplies inside already, so they went straight to the barn. The two of them stood around the pile of drop sheets, rollers, paintbrushes, and trays, staring at it.

"I'll be honest," Loretta said. "This is a lot more work than I thought it'd be. I understand if you want to back out." Dread crawled up her throat just looking at the multiple cans of paint.

"No way. We can do this. Small steps, right? Rome wasn't built in a day, and this barn is our version of Rome." Joyce rolled up her jacket sleeves and popped open a can of primer. "Point to a wall, and we'll start there."

Once they got going, Loretta's dread eased. After a few minutes, they propped the doors open to let in fresh air. "Something's missing," Loretta said, setting down her roller. "We need music."

She ran to the house to get her Bluetooth speaker. Back in the barn, she set it on one of the steps to the loft. "What type of music do you like?"

Without turning around, Joyce asked, "Do you have any David Bowie? Or T. Rex?" Just as Loretta suspected, those overalls hugged Joyce's ass in an unfairly flattering way.

"You're a glam rock girl. I like it." Loretta had a playlist that would work perfectly. She picked David Bowie's "Heroes" to kick things off, the familiar melody immediately boosting her mood.

Joyce bopped her head to the beat, revealing yet another side of her that Loretta hadn't expected. First the overalls, now dancing. Next it would be . . . Yes, Joyce could sing too. Not entirely on key, but she didn't seem to care.

Laughing, Loretta picked up her paint roller again and joined in.

The two of them sang and painted for a while, occasionally looking at each other with smiles on their faces. Energy filled Loretta in a way it hadn't in years; if not for her sore back and aching joints, she'd think she was twenty again. Especially with the music.

When "Bang a Gong (Get It On)" began, Joyce squealed and rushed over to turn up the music. Her dancing kicked up a notch, her body moving sinuously, her hips shaking, and Loretta found herself staring.

Joyce dipped her roller in the primer but got so caught up in dancing that she lifted it too soon, dripping primer down her arm. "Bollocks," she said, wiping at it. All that accomplished was getting primer on her hand, and she looked helplessly at Loretta, who burst out laughing.

"What's so funny?" Joyce asked. A piece of hair had fallen out of her bun, and she pushed it back with her arm, smudging primer on her forehead. "Well, shit."

Loretta laughed even harder and felt it in her abs, which hadn't seen this much activity in probably decades. "Do you need paper towel?"

Joyce stopped moving, her eyes narrowing. "You know, I don't think I do." Mischief sparked in her blue eyes, and she moved slowly toward Loretta.

"What are you doing?" Loretta asked, stepping back. The wall was another step behind her, and she couldn't move any farther or she'd run right into it.

"It's not fair for only one of us to make a mess," Joyce said.

"What do you—"

Joyce reached out, catching Loretta by the shoulder and smudging primer on her T-shirt and across her collarbone as she attempted to spin away.

"Joyce!" Loretta cried.

Joyce smirked. "We match now."

Game on. "I think I've got more than you. We need to even the scales." Loretta dropped her roller and picked up a paintbrush instead, dipping it in the primer.

"No, thank you, I'm good," Joyce said, backing up.

Loretta wasn't about to let her go that easily. "Oh no, you don't." She lunged forward and slapped primer on Joyce's back as Joyce shrieked.

"This is ridiculous!" Joyce yelled. But she laughed and picked up a paintbrush of her own, chasing after Loretta.

A few minutes later, the two of them collapsed on the floor, laughing. "I think there's more paint on us than there is on the walls," Joyce said.

"I think you're right." Loretta wiped tears from her eyes from laughing so hard. "We are the true masterpieces."

"Someone should put us in a museum," Joyce agreed. "I need water first though."

"Good idea."

Loretta pushed herself to her feet with some difficulty and pulled Joyce up from the floor, Joyce groaning loudly. They went inside and Loretta got them both water.

As they sat at the kitchen table in comfortable silence, catching their breaths and rehydrating, Loretta looked at Joyce.

The past hour in the barn had reminded Loretta of being young, goofing off with her friends in California. Going to parties, riling each other up.

Feeling that spark of connection with someone.

"Want a snack, then back to work?" she asked, redirecting her thoughts.

"Hmm?" Joyce had been looking out the window, her expression serene. She blinked at Loretta, smiling. That smile made Loretta feel things she thought she'd never feel again. "Oh, yes, that sounds lovely. If I can get these legs to work again."

Resisting the urge to push back the strand of Joyce's hair that had fallen forward once more, Loretta stood to get them food.

An image of Gail's face flitted through her mind, and she took a breath to steady herself. No matter how good being with Joyce felt, Loretta couldn't let herself get too comfortable.

CHAPTER FOURTEEN

JOYCE

*J*oyce couldn't remember the last time she'd felt so happy. She'd looked forward to seeing Loretta again, but she hadn't expected an impromptu dance party and a paint fight. Especially at their age. Surprisingly, she didn't care about the primer on her forehead, her arm, or her clothes, even if it did make her itchy. Sunshine filled her body, and even thoughts of Will and Andrew moving didn't upset her. She simply missed them and wished they could feel this too.

Whatever *this* was.

As she and Loretta headed back to the barn to continue painting after their snack, she tried to puzzle out her feelings, examining the pieces to get the bigger picture. She enjoyed Loretta's company and felt drawn to her. A magnetic pull, a desire to know all of someone's secrets purely so you could discover who they were on the most vulnerable level. The last time she recalled feeling this way was when she'd met Andrew, but that had been different.

Joyce mused on this as she rolled primer on the wall by the door, aware of Loretta painting only a few feet away. She'd pulled her hair back into a ponytail today, her curls wispy and swaying behind her as she moved. A few had fallen out and framed her face, giving her a youthful look.

When Joyce glanced over, Loretta was looking at her, her head tilted to one side and an expression of intense focus on her face. Joyce froze. "What is it?"

Loretta licked her lips, which were a soft pink close to Joyce's favorite color.

"Do you mind if I sketch you?" Loretta asked.

Joyce put her hand to her neck, unsure how to respond. No one had ever asked to sketch her before.

Loretta shook her head and laughed dismissively. "Never mind. I shouldn't have asked."

"You can sketch me if you want," Joyce said. She remembered Loretta's drawings of the barn, of her vision for the venue. They'd been stunning. If she could draw people with as much talent . . . Well, Joyce wanted to know how Loretta saw her.

"Are you sure? It's just . . . this light is really good, and you have a beautiful profile."

Did Loretta just call her beautiful? Or was that an artistic term?

Joyce cleared her throat, sure her neck was bright red. "Thank you. And I'm sure."

Loretta bit her lip, her eyes lit with excitement. "Okay, I'll be right back." She walked out of the barn, her steps light.

Joyce leaned out the doorway to watch her go, something stirring in her chest. This entire day felt like a dream, like she'd been transported back in time to the days when she dated more often. To the days when she picked up women without much thought, happy to fall in a semblance of love to forget her worries, then fall out of it, then do it all again a few weeks later.

She hadn't expected that to happen here, but if she read the signs right, Loretta showed interest in her beyond friendship.

A giggle slipped out between Joyce's lips and she covered her mouth, shocked at herself. She wiggled her body, trying to get rid of the giddiness bubbling through her veins before Loretta returned.

"Alright," Loretta said, coming in with a folding chair and her sketchbook. She unfolded the chair and sat in it, crossing one leg over the other. Splashes of primer covered her jeans, giving her even more artistic flair.

"Do I need to . . . pose, or something?" Joyce asked. She wanted Loretta to draw her, but she didn't know how to act under the spotlight. Loretta's gaze was almost tangible, as if she were lightly running her fingers over Joyce's brow, down her jaw, over her lips. Joyce tried not to shiver, tried to ignore the subtle pulse between her legs.

"No, no, keep painting. Pretend I'm not here. I mean, you can talk to me if you want. Just pretend I'm also painting."

Easier said than done, especially with Joyce's skin tingling under Loretta's artistic scrutiny.

"I'll try," Joyce said, turning her attention back to the wall.

Before settling down to draw, Loretta put the music on again. The first notes of "Ballroom Blitz" emerged from the speakers, and Joyce's nerves dissipated. Staying stiff and awkward wasn't possible with this song thrumming around them.

She relaxed, letting herself go loose as she painted, singing and having fun. Loretta sang too, not even looking at Joyce half the time when Joyce glanced over. And when she was looking, the two of them locked eyes, something passing between them like it had in the car on the drive from helping Minnie find her jumpsuit.

The music continued, one song rolling into the next, Joyce lost in the beat and her memories. She had no idea how much time had passed when Loretta said, "Would you like to see?"

Loretta's eyes sparkled, a smug smile on her face that made Joyce like her even more. Loretta may have been insecure about her business prowess, but she had no doubts about her artistic talent. That confidence pulled Joyce to her as if she and Loretta were magnets.

"Sure," Joyce replied.

While "Lonely Planet Boy" by the New York Dolls played, Loretta stood and Joyce met her to look at the sketch, standing just behind Loretta's shoulder.

"What do you think?" Loretta held up the sketchbook so Joyce could see better.

The breath whooshed out of Joyce's lungs. The portrait looked exactly like her, down to her slightly protruding chin and the wrinkles around her eyes. But the accuracy wasn't the most impressive part. Somehow, Loretta had captured joy on Joyce's face. Her head tilted back, her mouth parted, one shoulder up and the other down as if she were dancing. The sketch captured movement and *life*, like Loretta had created a snapshot of Joyce at her best.

"Wow," Joyce said, her voice breathy. "This is incredible."

She turned to Loretta only to find Loretta's face inches from hers. Light freckles dotted Loretta's cheeks, which Joyce hadn't noticed before. Her dark eyelashes cast shadows on her cheekbones, and without thinking about it, Joyce lifted a hand and touched Loretta's cheek.

Loretta sucked in a breath but didn't move.

Joyce didn't move either, her fingers hovering over Loretta's skin. "You are impossibly talented," Joyce said quietly.

"Thank you." Loretta leaned in, slowly, her nose almost touching Joyce's.

Joyce knew what that meant, what would come next. So many thoughts ran through her brain, and yet she couldn't grab a single one of them. They were all background noise compared to the woman in front of her.

Their lips touched, softly, and Joyce closed her eyes. The kiss didn't last long, but Loretta was still close when Joyce opened her eyes again. She cupped Loretta's cheek, this time lengthening the kiss, leaning into it, tasting Loretta. She was sugar and lavender and a hint of coffee.

The song switched, that moment of silence jarring Joyce out of the moment.

What was she doing?

She breathed in sharply and pulled back.

"S-sorry . . ." Loretta said, stepping back to put more space between them. "I didn't—"

"No, no, it's alright." Joyce held out a hand but didn't move closer. "I just wasn't expecting—"

"I know, me either."

Joyce wanted to explain herself, wanted to say she *enjoyed* the kiss, she just hadn't expected it to be so *tender*, but her phone rang. "It's Eleanor," she said, her heart pounding. "She's picking me up for dinner." She spun away from Loretta to answer the call, telling Eleanor she'd be out in a couple minutes.

She turned back to Loretta. "Listen, I—"

"It's fine, I understand," Loretta said, avoiding eye contact, her face bright red. "It won't happen again."

"That's not why I stopped."

Loretta's gaze flicked to hers, confused and pleading. But this wasn't the time to get into it—not with Eleanor waiting for her outside.

"I want to talk about this later," Joyce said firmly.

Loretta nodded. "Okay, okay."

They waved at each other awkwardly, then Joyce walked toward the car, only now noticing how stiff her joints were.

"How'd it go?" Eleanor said.

"Good." Joyce tried to pull her attention to the present, her mind still on kissing Loretta. She didn't usually lose herself in a kiss like that. "Yes, it went well."

Eleanor looked at her as if she expected more, but she shrugged when Joyce didn't elaborate. "That's good then."

"Mm-hmm."

Joyce looked out the window for most of the ride to Minnie and Eleanor's place, not really seeing the passing scenery. Loretta filled her thoughts. Her eyes, her lips, her freckles . . .

Next time, Joyce wouldn't pull away from the kiss.

CHAPTER FIFTEEN

LORETTA

 *W*hat the hell had just happened? Loretta had been having the best day with Joyce, and she'd drawn one of the best portraits of her artistic career. It wasn't finished yet, but the bones of it were there. She looked at it, one hand holding her sketchpad and the other on her lips, the softness of Joyce's mouth lingering there.

Almost two decades had passed since she'd kissed someone like that. And thoughts of Gail paled in comparison to the emotions currently taking over Loretta's body. Her heart raced, and yet she felt stuck in place.

Joyce had ended the kiss abruptly—as if it were a mistake.

Loretta couldn't parse out who had started things, but hadn't Joyce leaned into it? No matter how hard she tried, Loretta couldn't deny the attraction between them. Not only on a physical level, but how much they seemed to understand each other and enjoy each other's company.

So why had Joyce stopped the kiss? What was it about Loretta that pushed people away?

At least Joyce wanted to talk about it later . . . whatever that meant.

Shutting off the music, Loretta began cleaning up the paint

supplies. The silence made her thoughts louder, but for once, she didn't want to ignore them. Her feelings for Joyce sat solidly in her chest, the strongest thing Loretta had felt in ages. It scared her.

Maybe it scared Joyce too.

Maybe space was the best thing for both of them right now.

72 DAYS UNTIL THE WEDDING

Loretta didn't hear from Joyce for the next two days, which didn't help her anxiety. She cleaned her house from top to bottom to work off steam, and she assured herself that Joyce was probably busy.

Matthias and Evvie came over on Tuesday for dinner, and Loretta went to their place on Wednesday for brunch. Both days, Matthias asked where her brain had escaped to.

She hadn't told him about the kiss, and she wasn't sure she wanted to.

Loretta tried not to get too invested in whatever she'd started with Joyce—Joyce might not be interested. And Loretta wasn't looking to get into another relationship.

But every time she thought of how Joyce danced, how she laughed, how she could be both impeccably put together and relaxed enough to sing off key at the top of her lungs . . . Loretta wanted to spend more time with her. To get to know her better. To learn her favorite foods, her favorite animal, her favorite color. To discover what made her tick. What made her smile.

On Thursday morning, her phone rang as she was washing dishes with Persephone exploring the kitchen floor behind her. Loretta's heart leaped into her throat at Joyce's name on the screen, and she almost tripped over Persephone on her way to grab the phone.

"Hello?" Loretta wiped her hands on a towel, suds dripping

down her arm from where she held the phone. Persephone squawked indignantly as a few droplets landed near her.

"Good morning," Joyce said, her voice cheery as ever. "How are you doing?"

They went back and forth with typical small talk for a couple minutes, which made Loretta want to scream. Small talk was the bane of her existence, even more so with the awkward kiss situation hanging between her and Joyce.

"So," Joyce said, "I think I may have found the perfect light fixtures for the barn."

Multiple things ran through Loretta's mind at once. First, Joyce had the most soothing voice she'd ever heard, and she wanted to listen to it all day. Second, were they going to pretend they hadn't kissed each other? Joyce had said she wanted to talk, but she was acting like nothing had even happened. Third, light fixtures!

"Really? Where'd you find them?"

"They're at an antique store in Richmond. I've already asked Dylan if we can borrow her truck to go pick them up if you approve. We'd have to go tonight, though—apparently the owner is going on vacation tomorrow. I emailed you photos."

Once again, Joyce had given Loretta so much to absorb. Not only had she found potential light fixtures, but she wanted to join Loretta to pick them up. And she'd already arranged their transport. This woman was something else.

"One second." Loretta went to the living room and opened her laptop to check her email. Joyce had, indeed, sent her photos. Three round antique gold chandeliers—classic and understated— each with three tiers. Glass leaves adorned each tier, catching the light and making them look like something out of a fairy tale. Loretta struggled to judge their size from the photos, but they looked perfect for the barn. "These are beautiful."

"So you want them?"

"I do."

"Great. Would you be able to pick me up after lunch?"

Usually, Loretta wouldn't agree to go somewhere last minute —she preferred to have a few days to prepare—but she hadn't seen Joyce since they kissed. She wasn't about to turn down this opportunity to figure out where they stood. Plus, she couldn't wait to get those chandeliers.

"Yes, I can be there at two."

"Great. See you then." With that, Joyce hung up.

~

LORETTA'S HEART fluttered as she waited in the car outside the inn for Joyce, wondering what their dynamic would be like now.

Joyce looked like her usual professional self as she emerged from the inn in a skirt suit, her briefcase in hand. "Hello," she said cheerily as she stepped into the car. She didn't hold Loretta's gaze, quickly buckling herself in.

"Hey." If Joyce wasn't going to bring up the kiss right away, Loretta wouldn't either. Even if the thought of it was burning a hole in her chest.

They stayed quiet as they picked up Dylan's truck. Joyce stood back as Darcy and Bingley—Dylan's dogs—gave them an overenthusiastic greeting complete with dog slobber. Loretta thanked Dylan, then they were off.

"So, how've you been?" Joyce asked.

Loretta couldn't tell if that was a leading question. "I've been alright." Not really, but what else was she supposed to say? "I hope you don't mind—I hired someone to finish painting the barn. I thought it would take us too long." She'd also been scared that Joyce wouldn't want to continue painting with her after what had happened.

"Oh. Well, it did take an entire afternoon to paint that tiny section by the door."

"We probably would have got more done if we'd focused on painting the walls rather than each other," Loretta said, glancing at Joyce. Her heart fluttered like a nervous bird in her chest.

The smile that grew on Joyce's face put Loretta at ease.

"But primer really works with your skin tone," Joyce replied. "I couldn't resist."

"It's the new top makeup line, didn't you hear? Fifty shades of primer."

Joyce cackled.

The atmosphere in the car felt less charged after that. Conversation flowed easily again, as if the two of them had been friends for ages. Joyce told Loretta about how she'd gone to Kat's birthday dinner on Tuesday, then to Minnie's wedding outfit fitting the day before, which explained why she hadn't called. She truly had been busy.

"This is it," Joyce said after almost two hours of driving, pointing at a store with brick walls and peeling paint on the awning. "The owner should be expecting us."

The owner, a gentleman who looked to be in his sixties with tufts of white hair growing out of his ears, welcomed them heartily when they stepped inside. Joyce explained who they were, and he led them to a room upstairs. The chandeliers hung from the ceiling, all three in a line, and as soon as Loretta saw them, she knew they had to buy them.

"You're right," she said to Joyce. "These are exactly what I'm looking for."

Joyce beamed, and the owner called his two sons to help load the fixtures into the truck.

While they packed the chandeliers into boxes with packing peanuts, Joyce and Loretta went for dinner at a tiny, dingy café next door. Loretta grumbled about the state of the place, but Joyce said, "Some of the best food comes from little places like this. Don't judge it until you try it." And she was right; the café had homemade chips and salsa that Loretta would happily eat again.

When they went back to the antique store, the owner said, "We put a tarp over the top for you. Looks like rain any minute now."

They thanked him and got in the car, Loretta's eye on the sky. Dark clouds had rolled in while they'd been inside, the air too still and warm.

"Better drive fast," Joyce said, frowning as she looked through the windshield.

Loretta never went more than ten kilometers over the speed limit; she'd never gotten a ticket in her life. "I'll try."

Mere minutes later, rain crashed on the truck roof, so loud they couldn't hear the radio. "Shit," Loretta said, slowing. Within seconds, they were driving through massive puddles, Loretta's knuckles white on the steering wheel. "I think we should stop," she said. "I can't drive in this."

Joyce nodded. They pulled into a gas station parking lot, and Loretta checked the weather on her phone. She groaned. "This is supposed to last overnight. It's a severe weather warning."

"Sorry, what was that?" Joyce tapped her ear. "I turned down my hearing aids." She leaned closer as Loretta repeated herself.

They sat without speaking for a minute, resigned, listening to the rain and the thunder booming overhead. Loretta listened, anyway. Joyce had fiddled with her hearing aids again as they sat there, potentially turning them down even more.

"Should we find somewhere to stay the night?" Joyce asked.

Loretta sighed then said, loud enough for Joyce to hopefully hear her, "I don't think we have an option, unless we want to sleep in the car."

"I'd rather not."

At least if they were caught in a storm, they were caught in it together. If Loretta had been by herself, she'd have been panicking. But with Joyce beside her, the situation didn't seem so bad.

CHAPTER SIXTEEN

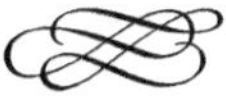

JOYCE

*J*oyce wasn't a stranger to rain, but she also didn't find herself caught in storms like this very often. Usually when it rained in Scotland, the clouds didn't sound so angry. Loretta kept calm though, which soothed Joyce's frazzled nerves.

They hadn't reached the highway yet, thankfully, and Loretta drove slowly along the streets, looking for a hotel or a B&B—anywhere they could stay that would keep them dry. She pulled over again, checking her phone for nearby places.

"There's one up here somewhere," she said, squinting through the rain as the car crawled forward. Joyce watched her lips as she spoke; she'd turned her hearing aids down so the thunder didn't sound as intimidating.

She glanced over her shoulder at the truck bed every few minutes, making sure the tarp was secure. Those chandeliers were important to Loretta, and Joyce didn't want them getting wrecked.

"Here it is."

They pulled up to a house surrounded by flowers in multiple colors, all hunched under the rain. Many of them would likely have their petals shredded by the morning. A pretty pastel sign on the porch railing stated the home was a B&B, but Joyce couldn't make out the name through the downpour.

Loretta sighed as she looked up the pathway. "There's nothing for it," she said. "We'll have to run."

"On a count of three." Joyce pulled her suit jacket as closed as it would go, preparing herself for the onslaught. "One . . . two . . . three!"

They burst out of the car, and Joyce's feet got soaked immediately from landing in a puddle. She shrieked. With their hands held fruitlessly over their heads, they bolted to the front door, panting and shivering as they rang the doorbell.

A small boy with dark hair sticking up in spikes answered. He took one look at them then shouted, "Mom!" over his shoulder. He stepped back and gestured with his arm. "Come in."

"Thanks," Loretta said, her teeth chattering. Odd how it could be so warm out then suddenly freezing as soon as you were drenched.

She and Loretta huddled together in the entryway by a small wooden podium that presumably acted as the front desk. Joyce turned her hearing aids up again slightly then pressed her shoulder into Loretta's, for warmth and for solidarity.

A woman, also with dark hair, came around the corner. "Hello," she said, pity in her smile. "Welcome to The Marigold." What was it with people around here and naming their inns after flowers? Joyce didn't care what the place was called, though, as long as it had hot water and a shower. "Got caught in the storm?"

They both nodded.

"We've got one room open right now, if you're looking to stay the night. It has a double bed and an attached bathroom. Breakfast included, and we'll make sure it's hot."

Loretta glanced at Joyce, and she nodded. They could share a room. And a bed. They were grown women who respected each other. They still had to talk about that kiss, of course, but Joyce hadn't found the right moment yet and Loretta hadn't brought it up.

"We'll take it," Loretta said, pulling her credit card out of her soggy purse.

"I'll pay you back," Joyce said, but Loretta waved her off.

Five minutes later, they stood in a room mostly taken up by a double bed. A wooden dresser ran along the left side of the room under a window, partially covering the closet, and the loo door was at the foot of the bed.

Once the hostess left, Loretta said, "There's barely any room to move in here. How'd they get the bed in?"

"It's not too bad." Joyce shuffled to the bottom of the bed. The bed that she and Loretta would have to share. They definitely needed to talk about the kiss before that, especially since Joyce wouldn't mind if it happened again.

Living up to the inn's name, the quilt was patterned with mustard-yellow marigolds.

"We could try to find somewhere else," Loretta said, her nose crinkled as she looked around.

A crack of thunder sounded overhead, and Joyce felt it in her bones. "I think that's a sign that we're better off here."

Loretta peeled off her soaked cardigan, revealing a black tank top that clung to her petite body. Joyce hadn't seen her in so few clothes before, or such tight ones. Her collarbone was fully on display, and Joyce bit her lip, averting her eyes. A bolt of heat shot between her legs. Collarbones had always been her weakness.

Following Loretta's lead, Joyce took off her suit jacket, draping it over a bedpost. She shivered, her skin damp. She wanted to change, but what would she change into? Neither of them had brought extra clothes or pajamas. She hadn't brought the charger for her hearing aids either. This wasn't meant to be an overnight trip.

"Do you mind if I shower?" Joyce asked. At least that would warm her up. And give her an excuse to stop staring at Loretta's bare skin, which she wanted to run her hands over.

"Go ahead," Loretta said. She looked ill at ease, standing between the wall and the bed in her wet clothes.

Joyce wanted to say something to improve the situation, but nothing came to mind. Rubbing her arms, she went to the loo and shut the door.

There wasn't much more space in here. The toilet fit snug between the sink counter and the bathtub, which had a shower curtain patterned—obviously—with marigolds. Joyce did her best to strip without banging her elbows on things, then she took out her hearing aids and hopped into the shower, letting the hot water wash away her shivers.

It couldn't wash away her nerves, though. As soon as she got out of the shower, she needed to talk to Loretta about that kiss. They were stuck in a tiny room with each other for the night, neither of them with any dry clothes, and Joyce couldn't lie beside Loretta in bed without clearing the air.

Although she dreaded leaving the shower's warmth, she didn't want to hog the hot water, so she turned it off. Thank the lord, the inn provided housecoats; two of them hung on the back of the bathroom door. The fabric scratched her skin lightly, but it'd do better than Joyce's wet clothes.

"They've got robes," she said, opening the loo door. She halted at the sight of Loretta sitting on the bed in her knickers and tank top, her jeans draped over the headboard.

Loretta's face lit up like a red lightbulb. "I couldn't sit in my wet jeans," she said. "They were giving me a rash."

"Mm-hmm." Joyce forced her eyes to the wall and held out the other robe.

Loretta took it from her and squeezed around her into the loo, closing the door softly.

Pulling her robe tightly around herself, Joyce shuffled around the bed and sat on the opposite side of where Loretta had been.

Seeing Loretta in only her knickers . . . a fizzy feeling zipped through her, her skin heating even more than it had under the hot water.

While she waited for Loretta to finish, Joyce went through her briefcase, making sure the contents had stayed dry. The edges of a few papers were wet, but that was it. Her pink notebook was safe. She leaned against the headboard, careful not to dislodge Loretta's jeans, and stared out the window at the sheets of rain still pouring down. Lord, what she wouldn't give for a hot cup of tea. What kind of inn didn't put a kettle in their rooms?

Her heartrate picked up when she heard the shower switch off and Loretta moving around. A soft "shit" and a *thump* made Joyce laugh, but she managed to keep her features neutral when Loretta emerged wearing her own white robe.

They locked eyes, the energy in the room charged with something unrelated to the storm raging outside.

Loretta sat next to Joyce, putting her legs out straight in front of her on the mattress.

"Well, at least we don't have to sleep in our wet clothes," Loretta said. The other option—sleeping naked—went unspoken between them.

"Loretta . . ." Joyce started, turning on her hip so she could look at Loretta more directly. "Can we talk about what happened? At the farm."

Loretta shifted too, mirroring Joyce and bringing them closer together. "What about it?"

Joyce looked at Loretta's long, thin fingers. Her eyes on Loretta's, she lifted one of Loretta's hands, holding it between hers. Even though she'd just had a shower, Loretta's skin was cold. Joyce wanted to pull Loretta close, to rub her arms and warm her up.

"I'm sorry," Joyce said, "for breaking off the kiss. I had suspected there was something between us, but I hadn't really thought through what could happen. Kissing you took me off guard."

Merely saying the words *kissing you* made Joyce want to do it again, especially when Loretta's gaze fell on her lips.

Loretta twined her fingers through Joyce's and shifted closer, so their knees touched. "I can understand that. So . . . I'm not terrible at kissing?"

A soft laugh bubbled out of Joyce. "No. Not at all. The opposite, in fact."

Loretta nodded and smiled coyly, her thumb moving back and forth over Joyce's knuckles in a soothing way. "You liked it?"

"Yes."

"Would you . . . do it again?"

Those lips. So soft, Joyce wanted to run her finger over them. "Yes."

She knew it was coming, but the kiss knocked the breath out of Joyce nonetheless. Loretta slid her fingers into the hair at the nape of Joyce's neck, and Joyce realized this was the first time she'd had her hair down around Loretta, free of its usual tight bun.

Their mouths moved together, Loretta's tongue gliding over hers, Loretta's teeth nipping at her lip. Joyce's breath became shallow, and she gasped in surprise as Loretta shifted again, slinging a leg over her so she straddled Joyce's hips.

Joyce's hands went to Loretta's waist, and she barely stopped herself from sliding her hands beneath Loretta's robe and onto the bare skin of her ribs, her breasts. "Wait," Joyce said, pushing Loretta back slightly. "We can't . . . I need to tell you something."

She couldn't let things go further without setting boundaries. She liked Loretta, and she didn't want to hurt her.

Her chest rising and falling, Loretta leaned back, her weight on Joyce's thighs. The green of her eyes was darker than usual, her pupils large. Her brow furrowed in confusion, but she still held a longing gaze. "Okay," she said, climbing off Joyce's lap. She crossed her legs and sat facing Joyce, giving her space. "What do you need to tell me?"

"I want this," Joyce said, gesturing between them. "But I don't do serious relationships. Not anymore." Or ever, really. Her relationships with her family were the only ones she wanted to put that kind of effort into.

Loretta nodded slowly.

"I'm going back to Scotland a couple days after the wedding. If you want this too, that's where it has to stop."

After a few seconds, Loretta said, "So, this would be a fling. A short-term relationship. Is that right?"

"Yes. A casual relationship, friends with benefits . . . whatever you want to call it." No mincing words. Joyce had been down this path before, and she knew how messy it could be if the other person wasn't on the same page. "If that doesn't sit well with you, then we can't do this."

Loretta narrowed her eyes, staring out the window at the rain. After a few moments, a look of determination came over her. She grabbed Joyce's hand, flipping it over. "That's fine with me." She ran her finger over the lines on Joyce's palm, making Joyce shiver.

"You're sure?"

"I'm sure."

"Thank the lord." Joyce leaned forward right as Loretta leaned toward her. Their lips crashed together. Both of their robes were off in seconds, and Joyce ran her hands up and down the length of Loretta's bare spine. Loretta arched into her, the curve of her neck long and begging Joyce to nip at it.

Joyce didn't realize it was still raining outside until some time later when they were ready to sleep, burned out for the evening. Joyce settled on her side, Loretta behind her, her arm around Joyce's waist.

"Have you noticed that everything around here is named after flowers?" Joyce murmured sleepily.

Loretta snorted. "Does that bother you?"

"It strikes me as overly quaint, and that's saying something."

Laughing, Loretta pulled Joyce more firmly against her. She snuggled into Loretta, grateful that out of everyone she'd met in Juniper Creek, she'd grown close to this woman.

And they hadn't needed pajamas after all.

CHAPTER SEVENTEEN

LORETTA

71 DAYS UNTIL THE WEDDING

oretta awoke to the sound of drizzling with Joyce warm under her arm. It took her a moment to remember where they were and how they had gotten there, and she pulled Joyce closer to her gently, wrapped in a bubble of contentedness.

Joyce's words from the night before came back to her. Loretta hadn't really thought through the possibility of them being together before, and it made sense that Joyce didn't want anything serious. The more Loretta thought about it, the more she decided it worked for her as well. Their relationship had a deadline, meaning there was no possibility of getting hurt like she had with Gail. She could enjoy her spring without worrying about what came after because there was no after.

Joyce seemed to share her contentment when she woke up, smiling over her shoulder at Loretta and indulging her in a good-morning kiss. The two of them got ready for the day, both cringing as they put on their still-damp clothes. As promised, the innkeeper made a warm breakfast of oatmeal, tea, and coffee, and the two of them were on the road again before nine.

Though it made the air humid and smell like wet laundry, Loretta kept the heat turned up on the ride back to Juniper Creek. Joyce seemed grateful, holding her hands in front of the vents, a small smile on her face. They had the radio on low, and they glanced at each other occasionally with bright eyes. That *something* still passed between them, but Loretta had a better idea of what it was now.

Loretta pulled up in front of the Bluebell, loath to say goodbye to Joyce but looking forward to getting home and changing into dry clothes. "Thank you for finding these chandeliers," she said. "And for coming with me to pick them up."

Joyce grabbed Loretta's hand, squeezing her fingers lightly. "You're welcome. I'll see you soon?" Loretta nodded, and Joyce headed out into the chill spring morning air, birdsong floating through the open car door.

From there, Loretta dropped off the truck at Dylan's, switching to her own car. Dylan would bring the chandeliers to the farm later that day when Hugo, one of the assistant librarians, and his girlfriend could help unload them.

When Loretta arrived home, Matthias and Evvie sat at the kitchen table, drinking coffee. "Good morning," Loretta said.

"Well, aren't you chipper," Matthias said. "Was it a successful trip?"

"Yes, I'd say so." In more ways than one. "We got the chandeliers."

Evvie clapped. "Wonderful! When can we see them?"

"Wait until they're up. I need to call the electrician I hired to install them. Probably in a few weeks, after the painting is finished." She turned to Matthias. "You fed the girls?"

Matthias nodded. "Fed, cleaned, tried not to kick." He winked at her, but she glared in return. "Okay, sorry, I would never kick the goddesses. You're right, that was in poor taste. Did you take your pills?"

She rolled her eyes. "Yes, I had some with me." She always packed a couple of antidepressants in her purse since she'd forgotten them once years ago when she'd visited Matthias in LA. She'd had the worst withdrawal headache and brain zaps.

Her brother and Evvie stayed and had lunch with Loretta, then she went for a nap, tired from the events of the past two days. But in a satisfying way.

Later that evening, she sat sketching on the recliner, a charcoal portrait of Joyce sleep-rumpled in bed. Loretta bit her lip, thinking of the last person she'd slept with.

Leaving her sketchbook on the coffee table, she went to her room and pulled a box out of her closet. She hadn't opened the box in years, but she couldn't bear to get rid of it. She set it on her bed and lifted the lid, revealing stacks of drawings, loose photos, and a few photo albums.

All of them of her and Gail.

Photos of the two of them outside the bar where they met, arms slung around each other's shoulders, heads thrown back in laughter. At Disneyland, mouse ears on their heads as they stood in front of the castle. On the beach, Loretta in a polka-dot bikini and Gail in a frilly yellow one-piece. Eating ice cream. Hiking. Gesturing to their first shitty apartment.

Her chest ached as she looked through everything, but she knew without a doubt that the ache came from grief—the grief of losing something you loved but didn't want again.

She closed the box, pressing her hands flat on the top, aware of the years of memories under her fingers. Her relationship with Gail had been a significant portion of Loretta's history. She'd thought romantic relationships in general belonged to her past, but now she reconsidered. Being seventy-one years old didn't mean she couldn't have another chance at romance, even if that romance was a temporary one.

Temporary romances were all she was cut out for, anyway.

She returned the box to her closet and went back to her

sketchbook. Instead of picking up the charcoal again, she phoned Joyce.

"Hello?" Joyce sounded surprised but not unpleasantly so.

"Sorry for calling so late," Loretta said. "Would you like to go for dinner sometime soon?"

"Dinner . . . ?"

"As in, a date. A dinner date. Would you like to go on a dinner date—with me—sometime soon?" Loretta held her breath, fingers crossed that she hadn't imagined everything that had happened the previous night.

"Oh. Yes, I'd love to." No hesitation whatsoever.

A wave of relief flooded through Loretta. They made plans to go to a new restaurant in Chilliwack called Valley Vineyard that claimed to be "an experience" as well as a restaurant.

After they hung up, Loretta picked up her sketchbook once more and flipped to a blank page. Time to start a new drawing.

～

67 DAYS UNTIL THE WEDDING

On Tuesday, Loretta dug through her closet, looking for a suitable outfit for her date with Joyce that night. Jeans, a T-shirt, and a cardigan wouldn't cut it. The restaurant website said casual attire was acceptable, but Joyce's casual attire was formal compared to Loretta's. And Loretta wanted to look like she belonged with Joyce, like the two of them were a couple, not a client and employer.

She found a dark green shirt with a mesh overlay and lantern sleeves, and it seemed dressy enough to pair with her black jeans.

When she picked up Joyce, she was glad she'd dressed up. Joyce wore a long light green dress and a cream-colored shawl. Green seemed to be that night's theme.

"You look beautiful," Loretta said, holding the car door open for Joyce.

"Thank you. You do as well."

An air of formality surrounded them both, but it dissipated as soon as Loretta put on her glam rock playlist for the ride. Joyce seemed unable to resist dancing and singing, and Loretta admired how uninhibited she could be.

Valley Vineyard was smaller than Loretta had expected, but it lived up to its reputation as "an experience." Tall hardy wooden shelves stretched from floor to ceiling, separating the bar from the dining room. They waited on the bar side to be seated, trellises draped in vines providing the backdrop to their wicker chairs. A few minutes later, a waiter approached them and led them to the dining room, where plants hung from the ceiling in white pots between long industrial-style hanging lights.

"This is an interesting place," Joyce said, looking at the ceiling.

"It is," Loretta agreed, running her finger over a plant trailing down the shelf beside her.

The interesting theme continued as they ordered their drinks: a cocktail called an Earth Connector for Loretta, and a classic gin and tonic for Joyce. Both drinks had ice cubes somehow stamped with the restaurant's logo.

The menu absorbed their attention for a few minutes, but once they ordered, they focused on each other again.

"So, how did you and Eleanor meet?" Loretta asked. "I know you two have been friends for a while, but she never told me how you got to know each other."

Joyce smiled, her face almost glowing from the light above their table. "Well now, that's a tale. But it starts with meeting Will and Andrew, because I wouldn't have met Eleanor or Amara without them. I met Will at a gay club a couple years previous, then he met Andrew through his work. The three of us became inseparable, as you do with your friends in your early twenties. We lived in London at the time, all of us sharing a flat, and one day Will procured a little baggy of marijuana. No idea how he got it, but at the time we didn't care to ask questions."

Loretta raised her eyebrows, amused. She hadn't expected

Joyce to have a history with drugs, yet here they were. Whenever they spent time together, she learned something new.

Joyce's eyes sparkled. "Don't look so surprised. We got high—because what else would we do? And Will said there was a flower show on that would be fun. I'm surprised we got there in one piece because I'm almost positive that weed was spiked with something. I knocked into someone as we were walking around, and that someone turned out to be Eleanor. I can't remember what we talked about"—she frowned—"but whatever it was, we decided to continue our conversation over drinks. She was with Amara at the time, and the five of us became fast friends." A sheen of nostalgia had come over Joyce's words.

"So you've known each other even longer than I thought. How did you end up in Scotland?"

"Ah, that's *another* story." Joyce told her about trying to find work in London, about how she apprenticed with a wedding-planning agency while Andrew and Will went to school. "We wanted to live close to our friends, but Eleanor and Amara were moving to Scotland for Amara's job at the University of Aberdeen. Eleanor's from Stonehaven, anyway, so she was looking forward to living near home. Will got this idea that he and Andrew could open a business together, but there was so much involved financially, and we were thinking about having a child together . . . One of Will's father's friends got us in contact with a man selling his boat in Macduff. Long story short, we moved up there to open the business."

They paused their conversation as their food arrived.

"There were enough clients there for your business?" Loretta asked. She could imagine a young Joyce, bubbling with energy, zipping from wedding to wedding.

Joyce's expression faltered, and she shrugged. "Not really. I had to travel a lot for work, and Will took a part-time job at a grocery. It wasn't ideal, but it worked for all of us. The more popular I got, the more I could charge, and I started taking on higher-end weddings. That way I didn't have to travel as often."

"Makes sense." Minnie and Eleanor's wedding didn't fit the *high-end* category, but that didn't seem to bother Joyce. "Did you see Eleanor and Amara a lot, then? After you moved?"

"We tried to see each other at least once a month, but it was difficult. Especially once we both had kids. We went on vacation together every few years, though, which was nice."

Loretta used to have friends like that in California—friends she could travel with. They were also friends with Gail, though, and Loretta lost touch with them when she moved. It hurt to think about.

Joyce must have seen the pain on her face. "What's wrong?" she asked.

"Just thinking about my own past," Loretta said. "I miss the people I had that type of bond with. But life happens."

"Life does happen." Joyce sighed. "When you least expect it."

Those words hid something more specific, but Loretta didn't want to pry. They moved on to lighter topics—Eleanor's upcoming appointment for dress alterations, when the painters were coming to work on the barn, the landscaping consultation Loretta had booked—but Loretta could tell Joyce's mind lingered on their previous conversation.

As the waiter cleared their plates, Loretta asked, "Is everything alright? When you said life happens when you least expect it . . . it sounded like you were referring to something specific."

Joyce blinked up at the plants around them and refolded her napkin neatly. "It's just . . . all this talk about meeting Will and Andrew, about becoming friends with Eleanor, and starting our business . . . I didn't expect my life to change so drastically this late in the game." She smiled wryly. "But with Will and Andrew retiring, they've decided they want to live in Italy."

Italy sounded like a lovely place to retire, and Loretta didn't see the connection between Joyce's words and her tone. "Do you not want to move to Italy?"

"Oh, no, it's a lovely place." She downed the last of her second gin and tonic. "I would love to go with them, but . . . Tori is staying in Banff. I don't think I can leave her. Especially since she got in an accident a few years ago on the boat." Joyce blew out a breath.

Loretta's chest ached in an echo of what Joyce must have felt. "Have you talked to her about it?"

"I have. She thinks we should all go, really. But I told her I don't want to leave her, and she said she'd be happy with me staying, too. Ideally, she'd live with us in Italy, but she's attached to the *Guillemot*. You couldn't pry her off it if your life depended on it."

Loretta took Joyce's hand across the table and squeezed it gently. "I'm sorry. Making that choice must have been difficult."

"It was, and I don't think it will stop hurting any time soon," Joyce said, rubbing a spot on her chest as if it ached.

"Pain often lasts longer than you wish it would. I understand that."

"You do?" Joyce's mouth turned down.

The waiter came by to take their dessert orders, but they declined, neither of them in the mood for something sweet. Loretta ordered tea, though, and Joyce coffee.

Loretta hadn't planned to tell Joyce about Gail, but maybe Loretta's story could provide Joyce some comfort. Thinking about Gail didn't hurt as much now; that much was clear after she went through her box of photos and sketches. She could put Gail's memory firmly in the past—the pain of it had finally dulled.

But she could dig up that past one more time for Joyce.

CHAPTER EIGHTEEN

JOYCE

Telling Loretta about Will and Andrew moving had hurt, but in some ways, it was also a weight off Joyce's chest. The more people she told, the more people she had to lean on. Not to mention that having someone understand you could provide a relief like no other.

"I think I just recently moved past the pain of my last breakup, which happened ages ago," Loretta started. She'd put her hair up in a half-bun tonight with a pencil keeping it in place, and it made her look artistically elegant. "My ex ruined the idea of romance for me."

"Really? But you're opening a wedding venue."

Loretta laughed quietly. "I know. I still love weddings somehow, no thanks to Gail."

Joyce held her mug of coffee right in front of her lips, inhaling the comforting nuttiness of it as she listened. She could tell this mattered to Loretta.

"I haven't talked to her for almost two decades, and we'd been together for that long as well."

Wow. "What happened?"

"We met in California, when I first got my job in tech. The first company I worked at was shit. The owner was a sadistic, homophobic, sexist prick, and every day I came home miserable. I found this bar—it wasn't really a queer bar, but it was a gathering place for queer people anyway. It was called Nectar & Ambrosia, and I started going there every day after work. They had fantastic drinks, and I made a lot of friends there. Including Gail."

Something pinged in Joyce's brain. "Sorry . . . Nectar & Ambrosia?"

"Yeah, yeah. The whole place had a Greek mythology theme. White pillars, a sky painted on the ceiling, drinks all themed after gods and goddesses. Even the bathrooms followed the theme. I remember the signs on the door for the women's washroom said 'Hera' and the one for the men's said 'Zeus.'" She snorted. "They tried to get the bartenders to wear togas, but that didn't last long."

Joyce couldn't help but laugh. "Is that why your hens are named after goddesses?"

"It is." Loretta huffed out a laugh. "I have a hard time letting go of things."

"There's nothing wrong with a little sentimentality," Joyce said, putting down her drink. She couldn't tell if she'd said that to comfort Loretta or herself more.

"I guess."

When Loretta quieted, likely drifting into her memories, Joyce prompted, "So you met Gail there?"

"Yes. Like me, she was unhappy at work and had found her escape there. The two of us saw each other almost every day for weeks, and without really talking about it, we started dating. We moved in with each other after a couple months, and we had all the same friends. She knew me better than anyone else."

Joyce had a feeling she knew where this was going, and her heart went out to Loretta.

Loretta stirred her tea, although she hadn't added anything to it. She likely needed something to do with her hands.

"Like I said, we were together for twenty-one years. Twenty-one years of sharing our hopes and dreams, buying a house, even getting a dog. I thought she was my forever, you know? She knew

I didn't want to stay in tech; once we had enough money, I wanted out. I wanted us to get our own hobby farm. Every time I brought it up, she indulged me in the vision, but she never seemed to take me seriously. That should have been a clue that we weren't aligned, but I ignored it. Then right before I turned fifty, my mom got sick. She hadn't been doing well, and she needed help on the farm. Matthias was in a band, so obviously the responsibility fell to me to help her."

Joyce didn't think that was so obvious, but they could discuss that later.

"When I brought up the idea of moving to Canada, at least temporarily, Gail looked at me like I had lost my mind. We fought a lot over it. Eventually, I realized she wouldn't come with me. She admitted she had no desire to live on a farm and no desire to live with or near my mother, no matter how accepting Mom was. No matter what compromise I came up with, she turned it down. I eventually had to accept that we didn't want the same things, even after so many years together. So we broke up."

Joyce wanted to hug Loretta, to do something to show her support. Something more than sitting on the other side of the table, nodding. It was her turn to reach for Loretta's hand, and Loretta gave it without hesitation. "And you haven't talked to her since then?"

She shook her head. "I've thought about it a lot in the past twenty years, and I admit that I saw our breakup coming on some level. I'd been feeling less connected to Gail, like she was slowly pushing me away. Every time we had an argument, she would pin it on me. And the night before I left . . . she told me she couldn't believe I would throw away everything we had to help my mother on our 'dinky little farm in the middle of nowhere.' As if my family didn't matter. As if what I wanted didn't matter."

Joyce inhaled sharply, hot anger rising in her throat.

"I truly thought she would go with me, but . . . I guess I wasn't worth following."

At those words, Joyce couldn't stay silent, although she kept her tone soft. "Loretta . . . Gail made a choice to stay. No matter what her reasons were, she had no right to belittle your dreams and values." She squeezed Loretta's hand, still in her own. "You *are* worth following, and Gail is a fool for not seeing that."

The corners of Loretta's mouth ticked up, her gaze on their connected hands. "Thanks. I don't even know if she really meant it, but what she said stuck with me." She let go of Joyce's hand and fiddled with her napkin instead. "Anyway. The pain of losing her, of wondering if I ever really knew her or if she ever really loved me, clung like a burr. But it did hurt less over time. And I'm sure that Andrew and Will moving away will hurt a lot now, but you'll get used to a new normal. And you'll be able to visit them, right?"

"Right." Joyce couldn't help but feel slightly irked at the similarities between her and Gail—both staying behind while their loved ones moved on. But it wasn't the same. Joyce was staying for her daughter, and Andrew and Will respected her choice. They were all on the same page. Not to mention that Joyce would *never* speak to her loved ones the way Gail had spoken to Loretta.

"I wish you didn't have to go through that pain," Joyce said. "But I'm glad you and Gail broke up."

Loretta narrowed her eyes. "You are?"

"Yes. You deserve so much better than that." She sat up straighter. "And now you're free to have fun with me."

"Well, when you put it that way . . ." Loretta replied, a smirk hiding at the corner of her mouth.

They paid their bills then headed out to the car. On the way to the inn, Joyce kept glancing at Loretta, light flickering over her as they passed streetlamps and other cars. Neither of them said much, but they could exist in that space comfortably with each other now.

When they pulled up to the B&B, Loretta insisted on walking Joyce to the door. "Like a true gentleman," she said with a wink.

Standing in front of the Bluebell's navy front door, Loretta hugged Joyce with just the right amount of pressure. Her hair smelled like springtime, a scent Joyce liked more and more each day.

"Can we promise each other something?" Joyce asked.

Loretta pulled back to look at her, the two of them grasping each other's arms.

"Maybe. What're you thinking?"

It might have been foolish for Joyce to want this, but she'd been longing for a sense of assurance since she left Scotland. Loretta had become an important part of her world in Juniper Creek, and after their conversation over dinner, she wanted to keep their relationship sacred. She wanted to show Loretta how much she mattered.

"Can we promise to stay on good terms with each other no matter how this thing shakes out? I don't think either of us needs more pain in our lives."

Joyce cringed at how much her question sounded like a vow. She'd been in the wedding industry for too long, clearly. Loretta didn't seem bothered, though. She nudged Joyce's toe with her own.

"I promise we'll stay on good terms," she said, not blinking as she stepped closer.

"Thank you." Joyce's words were so quiet, they were almost a whisper. She raised her voice as she said, "Me too."

With a smile, Loretta ran her hands down Joyce's shoulders. "Thank you for a wonderful evening." She leaned forward and pressed a kiss to Joyce's mouth, the softness of it making Joyce's stomach dip.

They said goodnight, grasping hands for a second then sliding their fingertips along each other's palms as Loretta moved down the steps. She waved as she got in her car, and Joyce went inside the B&B.

The lobby was empty, and Joyce sank into one of the couches, taking a moment to reflect on the evening before she headed up to bed. She'd come to Juniper Creek to help Eleanor and Minnie, and then she'd found Loretta. Her life had shifted in more ways than one in the last month and a half, but she liked this shift.

Will and Andrew had made plans without her, and now—for the first time in a long time—her life was changing without them.

But the future didn't scare her as much when she pictured Loretta by her side. At least, until the wedding.

CHAPTER NINETEEN

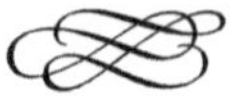

LORETTA

She and Joyce may have agreed to keep their relationship casual, but their date held significance for Loretta. Joyce's assurance that Loretta was worthy of following, that she deserved better than Gail . . . it almost brought Loretta to tears. She hadn't known how much she'd needed to hear those words until Joyce had said them.

And then Joyce had requested the promise afterward—that they stay on good terms after everything. That meant a lot too.

Loretta hadn't had a casual relationship before, and it was starting to sink in that she needed to keep a lid on her feelings. She could indulge them only enough to enjoy herself for the next few weeks, but then Joyce would be gone and they had to stay friends.

New terrain like this simply meant practice, and she had plenty of opportunities to hone her skills over the next few weeks.

The two of them saw each other multiple times as preparations for the wedding amped up. They met with Minnie and Eleanor to work on the seating chart and centerpieces—bouquets, of course, what else? Joyce made sure they had tables and chairs reserved for the rehearsal dinner and wedding day, and she helped Loretta direct the landscapers on the farm. They finished setting up Loretta's website together, including a contact form that

Loretta hoped would result in a client soon. They also spent a few days shopping for wedding decor, which was more fun than Loretta had expected.

Even when they weren't focused on the wedding, they went out for lunch and dinner together. Joyce visited the farm more often under the guise of seeing the goddesses, but the two of them always ended up watching nature documentaries, snuggled on the couch under Loretta's weighted blanket.

They learned more of each other's bodies as well, mapping their curves and wrinkles, getting to know each other's scars and birthmarks and the stories behind them. Loretta learned exactly where to kiss Joyce to make her whine low in the back of her throat, and Joyce learned how to make Loretta see stars and crest waves of pleasure she'd never ridden before. Joyce seemed determined to show Loretta just how much she'd been missing with Gail and in the years since her breakup.

⁓

46 DAYS UNTIL THE WEDDING

Passover had started the day before, and in all the hubbub Loretta hadn't seen Joyce for a couple of days. Her nerves were on edge, like part of her was missing and she needed to get it back. Even Matthias noticed when he and Evvie came over for dinner before they were set to fly to LA. While neither Loretta nor her brother celebrated the holiday in full, they always made sure to mark the occasion in memory of their parents and to honor their heritage.

Now, they stood at the counter making matzo balls for the soup they'd eat later that evening. Loretta had dug out their mother's recipe and had all the ingredients ready on the counter: eggs, vegetable oil, vegetable stock, matzo meal, nutmeg, ginger, and parsley. She measured each one while Matthias stirred them together; the mixture had to chill for a few hours before they could form the matzo balls.

"So, you've been seeing Joyce a lot lately, hey?" he said, covering the bowl in saran wrap.

Loretta knew what he was getting at, but he'd have to dig if he wanted details. "Yes. There's a lot to do with the wedding coming up. Just over a month left to go!"

"Yeah, yeah, the yard is looking good. We should have put a fence in sooner." He stuck the bowl in the fridge. "You've been talking about Joyce a lot too."

"Okay. So?" She tried to hide her smile by putting the spices in the cupboard. Of course she'd been talking about Joyce a lot. She enjoyed spending time with her.

"So . . . is there something going on there that I should know about?"

She glanced at her brother. "Maybe."

"I knew it!" Matthias pumped a fist in the air. "My baby sister has a girlfriend!"

Loretta snorted. Could one still be called a *baby sister* when they were seventy-one years old? "She's not my girlfriend. We're only together until she leaves after the wedding."

Matthias looked taken aback. "Sorry, what?"

"It's just a fling."

He blinked at her. "A fling? Loretta, you don't do flings."

"Says who?"

"Um . . . everyone who knows you well? You've never done casual *anything*. You don't even like small talk."

"Well, there's a first time for everything. This is my first fling."

He raised his eyebrows. "Okay, okay. I mean . . . you don't really talk about her like it's a casual thing."

"What do you mean?"

"You talk about her as if she walks on water."

She scoffed. "I do not."

He laughed as he started washing the dishes. "Whatever you say. Regardless, I'm happy for you." He lightly shoved her shoulder with a soapy hand.

"Thanks."

Although she acted like he was annoying her, his enthusiasm made her happy.

They finished cleaning the kitchen together, and Matthias made them mugs of tea. It'd been raining all week, but the weather had given them a break that day, so they took their drinks outside to the bench where they could sit and watch the hens enjoy the sun.

For the rest of the day they talked about memories of their parents and how they would celebrate Passover when they were kids. Their dad had made the best potato kugel. And when they each turned ten, their mom had given them their own children's Haggadah. Loretta still had hers, but Matthias didn't know where his had disappeared to.

Evvie joined them for dinner, the three of them rolling out matzo balls together and adding them to the pot of boiling water. Matthias had the vegetable soup started already, and it wasn't long before they settled at the table with their meal.

"This is delicious," Evvie said around a mouthful.

"I like the chicken soup version better," Matthias said, "but *someone* had to go and become a vegetarian." His tone was light, and Loretta wasn't bothered.

She gave him a teasing glare. "You want me to eat chicken soup with the girls out back? You cruel and unusual man."

"I'm on Loretta's side with this one," Evvie said. "Although I do enjoy a good chicken soup."

As dinner continued, the conversation shifted to Evvie and Matthias's trip to LA. Matthias said, "We're going to celebrate Stephen's and Nick's birthdays on Sunday. Nick has something planned, but I didn't bother asking what it was."

Knowing Nick, the most spontaneous and lively member of Iridium Twilight, it'd be a rowdy party with all their friends and too-loud music. Loretta had been impressed at how tame Nick had been when he'd stayed with them over the winter holidays; that wasn't his MO.

"I'm glad we're staying with Stephen." Evvie wiped her mouth with a napkin. "He said we'll likely leave the party early."

Matthias nodded and leaned back in his chair, patting his full stomach. "As long as we get cake first."

"Obviously," Evvie agreed.

Loretta was glad Evvie would get to meet Stephen—Iridium Twilight's bass player—and Matthias's other friends in LA. She'd see pieces of his past that she'd only heard about so far, and Matthias even had a secret concert lined up for her. The trip would give them new memories to bond over for years to come.

As she watched her brother and Evvie chat more about their plans, a shade of jealousy tinged her excitement for them. She wanted to go on trips with Joyce, but after the wedding, they'd be only friends. Maybe Loretta could visit her sometime, or they could meet for a sort of vacation fling . . . if that was a thing people did.

Loretta thought she'd been doing well at keeping her feelings in check. She'd managed to keep Joyce's departure at the back of her mind until Matthias had brought it up. Now it kept poking at her.

She must have been frowning because Evvie put a hand on her arm and asked, "Are you okay?"

Loretta nodded and tried to get a handle on her thoughts. She was sure she could do the casual relationship thing if she tried hard enough. But . . . she wanted to see Joyce all the time. She wanted to hear her thoughts and opinions, to see her smile, to give her gifts that brought her joy, to take her places she hadn't been before, to experience as much as she could with her in the weeks they had together.

Damn. That sounded too much like love for Loretta's comfort.

She had fallen deeper than she thought.

CHAPTER TWENTY

JOYCE

39 DAYS UNTIL THE WEDDING

Joyce flipped another page in *H is for Hawk*, a book Loretta had given her because they both liked birds. She hadn't expected a book about taming a hawk to be so engrossing, but she couldn't put it down.

Her phone went off, and she smiled when she saw Loretta's name on the screen. She set the book aside.

"The lights are up!" Loretta said.

"The lights?" Half of Joyce's brain was still in the book.

"The chandeliers we got? They've officially been installed."

"Oh!" Joyce perked up. "I thought that was happening tomorrow?"

"I thought so too, but they showed up first thing this morning. I don't know which of us got the date wrong, but good thing I was home. Would you like to see them? I can come get you now if you're ready."

"Of course!" Joyce pulled herself away from reading to freshen up.

Fifteen minutes later, Loretta met her in the lobby. "I can't wait for you to see them," she said, kissing Joyce on the cheek.

"I can't wait to see them," Joyce replied, following Loretta to the car. They'd put together a playlist with their favorite rock songs the previous week, and Loretta turned it on. Music had always been part of Joyce's life, and now it drew her and Loretta closer together.

"Okay, close your eyes," Loretta said when they got out of the car. "I'll lead you over there, but I want you to get the full effect at once." She practically wiggled with excitement, and Joyce couldn't help but laugh at her. Loretta didn't often display her enthusiasm like this.

She grasped Loretta's hand. "Don't let me run into anything."

The landscapers had finished putting in the pathways, so they had smooth ground to walk on. No more mud to sink into or rocks to trip over. The entire farm looked much more wedding worthy now with the wooden rail fences built, the paths in place, and the bones of the gazebo up.

Joyce moved slowly. Even though she trusted Loretta to lead her, she didn't hold that same trust in her feet.

Finally, the air shifted around her as she stepped into the barn, careful to keep her eyes closed. She didn't want to deprive Loretta of her big reveal. The scent of fresh paint reached her nose, lingering from the new coat of white on the walls.

"Okay, stand here," Loretta said, moving Joyce by her shoulders. "Aaaand . . . open!"

Warm light filled Joyce's vision as she opened her eyes. The three chandeliers were mounted on the barn ceiling, hanging low enough to be noticeable but still high enough to be out of the way. The glass leaves sparkled, and the entire barn seemed transformed.

"Wow," Joyce said, her voice breathy. "They're beautiful."

"Aren't they?" Loretta wound her fingers through Joyce's and leaned her head on Joyce's shoulder, gazing at the lights. "This is exactly what I envisioned. We could add market lights if we want, but these would be fine on their own too. They make the whole space seem . . . cozy."

"Cozy and magical." Joyce leaned her head against Loretta's. It was as if the two of them stood in their own little world, in a space they'd brought to life together.

They stood there for a couple more minutes, then Loretta broke the quiet bubble surrounding them. "I snapped a photo and added it to the wedding board. Would you like to see?"

The wedding board lived at the farmhouse now. She and Loretta had been updating it together, adding a photo as each major task was completed. It looked fuller each week as the wedding drew closer, and Joyce loved seeing everything come together.

"It fits perfectly," she said, looking at the photo of the barn. Loretta had replaced the old mock-up photo, and the reality of the barn looked even better. "Eleanor and Minnie are going to love it."

"I hope so. I couldn't have done this without you, you know."

Joyce put her arm around Loretta, who leaned into her, returning the embrace. "You could have. You would have figured it out eventually."

"Maybe, but I might not have found those chandeliers."

"Maybe."

"Can I kiss you?"

Joyce nodded, trying and failing to suppress a grin.

Loretta kissed her, her lips so soft it made Joyce's heart ache. She kissed Loretta's forehead in return, glowing at the satisfied smile on Loretta's face.

"I got you something," Loretta said, pulling away.

"What? But you just showed me a surprise."

"Well, this is more specifically for *you*. And you don't have to close your eyes for this one." Loretta disappeared into her bedroom and came out a few minutes later with her hands behind her back. "I hope you like it," she said, revealing a puzzle box. The puzzle showed two puffins nuzzling each other.

"Two thousand pieces? That's ambitious. But I love it." And she did. Her heart fluttered. Loretta had seen this and thought of her. She knew Joyce well enough now to buy something tailored to Joyce's interests. Not to mention how Joyce had told her she should visit Scotland one day to see the puffins. That plan had become more concrete in Joyce's mind. She could easily see Loretta in a Mackintosh and wellies, crouching to watch the puffins go about their day on a rocky cliffside. Her resting bitch face would look impressively stoic against a gray Scottish sky, her thick curls blowing in the wind. "Can we do it together?"

"Now?"

"Why not?"

Loretta shrugged, and they cleared off the kitchen table. They worked on the puzzle well into the evening, taking a break for tea and another to finish a documentary they'd started a few days before. They'd gotten most of the border done, but the puzzle would clearly take hours longer. By the time Joyce thought to look at the time, it was already half nine.

"I'm sorry I stayed so late," she said. "I hadn't been paying attention."

"Me either," Loretta replied, waving her off. She licked her lips and shifted to face Joyce. "What if . . . I mean, you can say no if you want. But, would you be interested in spending the night?"

Joyce's heartbeat picked up. Not so much because of the implications—the two of them had been intimate a few times since The Marigold, usually on Loretta's couch or in her room—but because she hadn't planned this. She'd spent every night for the past two months at the Bluebell, and all her things were there. She didn't even have a toothbrush with her. Or her hearing aid charger.

And spending the night with Loretta meant something. Joyce knew they were more than friends, that much was obvious. But they were casual lovers. Staying the night may not have meant anything for most people, but for Joyce and Loretta, staying together overnight took things a step further. That said they enjoyed each other's company enough that they didn't want to part, even to sleep.

"You know what?" Loretta said in response to Joyce's silence. "Forget it. It was a bad idea."

Joyce bit her lip. She wasn't a risk taker, but she truly didn't want to leave. She didn't want to say goodbye to Loretta for the evening. "No. I'd like to stay."

"You would?" Loretta's face lit up. "I have a new toothbrush you can use in the cupboard."

A laugh bubbled out of Joyce. "You know me so well."

They read on the couch together—thank goodness Joyce had stuck her book in her bag—then headed to bed. Loretta's room smelled like lavender, like she did. A few cardigans hung over the desk chair, sketches lay scattered on the desk, and a stack of books stood crookedly on one night table. Coming in here always made Joyce feel at ease.

"Can I sleep on the left?" Loretta asked. "I almost always end up on that side."

"Of course. It's your house."

A sense of awkwardness permeated the air while they brushed their teeth and got ready for bed. Loretta gave Joyce one of her oversized band T-shirts to sleep in, the fabric so soft that Joyce wanted to curl up in it.

Once they got into bed, the awkwardness continued for a minute, both of them trying to figure out what was comfortable. Joyce wondered if staying had been a bad idea—maybe it took their relationship too far. She turned over once more at the same time as Loretta, and they smacked foreheads.

"Ow," they said in unison, then they burst into laughter.

"You know," Loretta said, rubbing her forehead, "I didn't think sharing a bed with you would be so difficult, especially since we've done it once before." Her tone was light, teasing.

"Me either," Joyce replied. "But I think I know how we can make it easier." She moved closer to Loretta, trailing her fingers up Loretta's bare thigh.

Loretta twined her fingers in Joyce's hair, her eyes dark. "That just might work."

A FEW HOURS LATER, Joyce lay awake in the dark, curled around Loretta. They'd flung their pajama shirts haphazardly on the floor in their eagerness to touch each other, and now they snuggled skin to skin. Every time Joyce shifted slightly, Loretta's tousled hair tickled her nose, but she didn't mind.

Loretta's breathing had slowed as she'd drifted off, but Joyce couldn't sleep. Her brain wouldn't turn off.

She and Loretta made a good team in multiple ways. They'd essentially been working as business partners on Eleanor and Minnie's wedding. They enjoyed watching nature documentaries together, they read the same books, they both liked puzzles. And now they were spending the night together, voluntarily.

As the wedding drew closer, so did her separation from Loretta. They'd agreed on it, and it's what she wanted, but as she imagined leaving this woman . . . That was just it—she couldn't imagine leaving her.

And yet, she would. She couldn't afford for her life to get any more complicated.

38 DAYS UNTIL THE WEDDING

Joyce must have fallen asleep because she woke the next morning in confusion. It took her a moment to realize she was in Loretta's room. Loretta had gone, the space in bed beside Joyce empty.

She stretched out, basking in the light lavender scent of Loretta's sheets. Wait until she told Will and Andrew that she'd slept in another woman's bed. Wait until she told *Tori*. The image of Tori's disgusted face popped into her head and made her laugh.

"What's so funny?" Loretta came to the doorway in her pajama shirt and slippers, two cups of coffee in hand.

"Oh, just thinking about how Tori would react if I told her I'd slept at yours last night. She'd be happy for me, but she'd act like I'd told her something filthy." She snickered.

Loretta laughed, the rich notes of her voice washing over Joyce. "If I told Matthias, I'm sure he'd be the filthy one about it." She handed Joyce one of the mugs.

"Thanks." Black coffee, exactly how Joyce liked it.

They spent an hour or so in bed, discussing their plans for the day. They had an appointment at the bakery that afternoon with Eleanor and Minnie to taste a few different cake samples Aaliyah had whipped up for them.

"This is one of my favorite parts of wedding planning," Joyce said. "Cake tasting. I always insist I don't need to try anything, but my clients usually say they need help deciding."

"They twist your rubber arm, hey?"

"That they do."

Loretta agreed to run Joyce back to the B&B so she could change her outfit. Sleeping in someone else's clothes was one thing, but dressing in them for the day was another. Loretta was too petite, anyway; there's no way Joyce could fit into her clothes, and she wasn't about to wear yesterday's outfit again.

Not to mention she needed to charge her hearing aids, at least for half an hour. She didn't want them turning off during the cake tasting.

"Should I wait down here?" Loretta asked when they arrived at the Bluebell.

"I don't have a problem with you coming up," Joyce said. "As long as you don't mess up my things."

"Oh, you know me," Loretta said, following Joyce up the stairs. "I can't resist rummaging through people's suitcases."

Joyce opened her room door with her keycard. "You think I left my things in my suitcase? What kind of heathen would that make me?"

"Right, sorry," Loretta said, laughing. "Of course you'd hang up all your clothes in a B&B. When'd you unpack? The day you got here?"

"The morning after, thank you very much." Joyce turned up her nose, but she couldn't resist smiling.

Loretta plopped onto Joyce's bed. "Does it feel weird to have someone else make your bed every day?"

"Oh, I make it myself before they come in. And I've told them not to change my sheets unless I request it."

"Why am I not surprised." The fondness in Loretta's eyes filled Joyce with warmth.

"Right, behave yourself," Joyce said before she closed the washroom door.

She'd just finished putting her clothes on and was running a brush through her hair when Loretta knocked on the door. "Joyce, your phone is ringing. It's Tori."

The blood drained from Joyce's face, and at first, she didn't understand why she felt so shaky. They usually scheduled their calls in advance, and their next one wasn't until Friday.

Then it came flooding back to her: She'd been helping a bride get ready for her big day in Mexico when Andrew had phoned to tell her about Tori's accident. Just like now, Joyce hadn't been thinking about her family at all. But Andrew had told her sit, then he'd explained that Tori had taken her boat out by herself and got caught in a storm. The coastguard had rescued her, but her ship was unsalvageable.

And Tori's trauma would change both her life and Joyce's for years to come.

Joyce fumbled to put in her hearing aids then opened the door, dread weighing on her. She couldn't feel her hand as she held it out to take the phone from Loretta.

"Hello?" she answered breathlessly.

"Hiya, Mum, it's me." At the sound of Tori's voice, a wave of relief rushed from Joyce's head to her feet. "I just got home from work and . . . I wanted to talk to you." Her words wobbled at the end.

Joyce sat on the bed. She could tell this call had a purpose. "Alright, I'm here."

Tori sniffed. "Sorry, I feel rather daft right now, needing to talk to my mother." She laughed, but it sounded forced.

"I'm always here for you, my dove, you know that. What would you like to talk about?"

"There was a storm today. We knew about it, but it wasn't supposed to hit until later, so we led a tour anyway."

Joyce sucked in a breath. Tori had been extra wary of storms since her accident.

"We got caught in it, and everything was fine really, except the waves were rough and three of the guests got seasick. I managed to keep it together, but now I . . ." Her daughter's breathing quickened over the phone.

Loretta shifted closer to Joyce, her hands out as if Joyce were about to fall and Loretta would catch her.

"You're alright, my dove, I'm here. I've got you." Joyce wanted nothing more than to be with Tori right then, to hold her tight and make her feel secure. The thought of the *Guillemot* getting caught in a storm made Joyce feel nauseous, and she hadn't even been on the boat.

Lord, Tori could have fallen overboard again. She could have been attacked by a whale. She could have hit a rock. She could have *drowned*.

"I know, I know, I'm okay. Just shaken. Can you stay on the phone with me for a bit?"

"Of course. I'll be here as long as you need me."

At some point, Loretta had put a hand on Joyce's arm. Her grip tightened at Joyce's words. "Is everything alright?" she whispered.

Joyce tilted her phone away and explained what had happened in a hushed voice. "She's okay, but she asked me to stay on the phone with her." She looked at her watch. "We're supposed to be at the bakery soon. Would you mind going without me?"

Loretta shook her head. "Of course not. Whatever you need. I can come check in after, if you want. Make sure everything's okay and fill you in on the cake tasting."

"Sure. Thanks."

After kissing Joyce's cheek, Loretta headed out to meet Eleanor and Minnie.

Joyce leaned against the headboard and asked Tori about mundane things like what she'd eaten for breakfast, trying to get her mind off the rough seas.

This was precisely why she couldn't live away from her daughter. Joyce was so helpless, sitting here on the other side of the world while Tori was on the verge of a panic attack. What if it had been something worse? What if she'd been in another accident? Joyce couldn't do anything from half a world away.

In that moment, she felt extra confident in her choice to stay in Scotland. She needed to be with Tori. She couldn't live away from her daughter.

CHAPTER TWENTY-ONE

LORETTA

*L*oretta didn't want to leave Joyce, but Joyce had asked her to go to the cake tasting, so she would. On her walk to the bakery, she thought about Tori, hoping she was truly alright. For her own sake, and for Joyce's.

As Loretta approached the bakery door, she saw the sign was flipped to "Closed." She stopped in confusion, but Aaliyah appeared on the other side of the door and opened it for her. The smell of fresh-baked bread embraced Loretta. She didn't go into town often, but when she did, she always visited the bakery.

"Come in, come in," Aaliyah said. As the main baker, Aaliyah usually had a spot of flour somewhere on her outfit, and Loretta couldn't remember ever seeing her without her apron. Today, though, Aaliyah wore jeans and a pink ruffled blouse, a silky dark teal hijab giving her a formal vibe. Had she put all this effort in for the cake tasting? Minnie and Eleanor would hire her regardless, but perhaps Aaliyah was like Joyce—everything had to be done the right way. "We closed the bakery for a couple hours for the cake tasting."

"Oh, you didn't have to do that," Loretta said.

"I know, but we thought it'd be easier. For us, and for the

brides." She had a point. "Kamran's getting the plates ready in the back. Go ahead and have a seat."

"Hello," Minnie said, waving at Loretta from a round table in the center of the bakery. Eleanor sat beside her, also smiling. Over the weeks since finding her wedding jumpsuit, Minnie had seemed to get progressively more relaxed. Loretta thought her nerves would have heightened as the wedding got closer, but maybe ticking items off the to-do list relieved her anxiety. "Where's Joyce?"

Loretta sat across from Minnie and Eleanor. "She got a call from Tori . . ." She explained the situation, assuring them that Tori was fine.

"Oh." Eleanor held her amethyst necklace as if it gave her comfort. "What an awful thing to happen, and after Tori's boating accident too. Joyce must be so worried."

Minnie nodded and grabbed Eleanor's hand.

"I'm sure it will all be fine, though," Loretta said. The wedding show must go on, and she had to keep it running in Joyce's stead. "For now, let's focus on cake, shall we?"

"Speaking of," Aaliyah said, coming over with a pot of tea and three mugs, "the first samples will be out in a minute."

The three of them prepared their tea, and Kamran emerged from the back room carrying three plates. "Here are your first samples," he said, as boisterous as ever. He set the plates in front of Minnie and Eleanor. "Red velvet with cream cheese frosting, white chocolate raspberry, and lemon raspberry." He grinned broadly.

Aaliyah came to stand near them, not hovering, but observing. "Let us know what you like and what you don't," she said. "We can always change things up."

"Goodness, how many samples are there?" Eleanor asked, picking up her dessert fork.

"There are three more," Kamran replied. "We wanted to provide options."

"Small bites only, I suppose." Minnie took a bite of the red velvet cake. "Loretta, you'll have to help us."

Loretta tried not to smile—Joyce had been right. "If you insist." She wouldn't say no to free cake, and she wondered if she could get a slice or two boxed up for Joyce.

The three of them tried the first samples, then Kamran brought out three more: vanilla with dulce de leche, pink champagne with Bavarian cream, and a classic carrot cake with cream cheese frosting.

"How on earth are we supposed to pick one?" Minnie groaned, her hand on her stomach. "They're all delicious!"

Loretta agreed, glad it wasn't her decision to make.

"The carrot cake has pineapple in it," Eleanor said, "and that's one of your favorites, isn't it?"

"Yes, but the others are amazing as well!"

Aaliyah laughed, clearly pleased with their feedback. "Should we bring out a few other options?"

"Oh, goodness no," Eleanor said, holding up a hand. "We can barely pick between these ones!"

As they debated which flavors they enjoyed the most, Loretta wondered how Joyce and Tori were doing. Joyce cared about her family more than anything else. Will, Andrew, and Tori came up so often in their conversations, Loretta felt like she knew them. She looked forward to meeting them when they came to town for the wedding.

A ball of dread formed in her stomach now, though. Joyce's renewed worry about her daughter would make her even more eager to go back to Scotland after the wedding. Loretta knew Joyce would leave—they'd both been counting on it—but things like this reminded her in no uncertain terms that she'd be losing Joyce.

She thought casual meant she'd avoid heartbreak, but Matthias was right. Loretta couldn't do casual.

All the cake in her stomach soured, and she pushed her plate away.

Minnie's voice interrupted her thoughts. "Loretta?"

"Hm?" Loretta looked up to find Minnie, Eleanor, and Aaliyah staring at her expectantly.

"Which one did you like better? The white chocolate raspberry, or the carrot cake?" Minnie asked.

Loretta had been too absorbed in her own thoughts to follow how they'd narrowed down the flavors, but from their previous reactions, she got the feeling Minnie wanted the carrot cake while Eleanor preferred the white chocolate. What would Joyce do in this situation?

A compromise. Something that would make both brides happy. "What if you did a smaller white chocolate raspberry cake, then did carrot cake cupcakes on the side? That way you can have both flavors."

"Oh!" Minnie beamed, and Eleanor clapped.

"That's a wonderful idea, Loretta," Eleanor said. She turned to Aaliyah. "Can you do that?"

Aaliyah nodded. "Of course. Guests can have options then as well, so everyone will be happy."

With the cake decided on, the three of them finished their tea. Kamran and Aaliyah sat with them, and Minnie and Eleanor asked about their sons. Had Rashid decided on a university yet? How did they feel about Adi's new girlfriend?

Loretta let the conversation wash over her, mm-hmming when necessary. Her mind was on Joyce, and she had to stop herself from running out of the bakery and back to the inn.

"Well, we shouldn't keep you any longer," Eleanor said eventually. "I'm sure people are waiting for their afternoon coffees."

Aaliyah boxed up the leftover samples for Loretta to take to Joyce, and they said their goodbyes. The next big event was the pre-wedding party in a couple weeks—which Minnie and Eleanor wanted instead of the classic bachelorette party and wedding shower—so they had time to relax.

Joyce would have time to relax as well—if she could after Tori's recent scare.

A light drizzle made Loretta's hair frizz as she walked to the inn, shielding the box of cake under her jacket. She went straight to Joyce's room and knocked lightly on the door.

Joyce had changed into yoga pants, a plain T-shirt, and a cardigan that looked suspiciously like one of Loretta's. The outfit change would have concerned Loretta, except Joyce didn't appear upset even though her eyes were tinged red. In fact, the corners of her mouth ticked up as she let Loretta in. After noticing the cake, she wrapped Loretta in a hug.

"So Tori's okay?" Loretta asked, handing her the cake box.

Joyce nodded. "She is. I'm still worried about her, but Burt is home now to keep her company."

"Good. I'm glad she's alright."

The two of them sat side by side on the bed, their legs crossed. Joyce popped open the box of cake. "Oh, you even brought me a fork!"

"Obviously," Loretta said. "I didn't want you eating it with your hands."

Joyce took her first bite and closed her eyes, humming in pleasure. "This one's good. What flavor is it?"

Loretta told her all about the tasting and what Eleanor and Minnie had decided. The rain picked up outside, droplets sliding down the window, and Joyce gave Loretta a knitted blanket to wrap around her shoulders.

Despite the coziness of the blanket and Joyce's seemingly good mood, the ball of dread remained in Loretta's stomach. She ignored it as best she could, focusing on the present and the beautiful woman right in front of her.

CHAPTER TWENTY-TWO

JOYCE

Joyce didn't have much to do for the wedding over the next few weeks, and she would have felt at a loss were it not for Loretta. The two of them spent so much time together at the farm, it had started to feel like home. They'd finished the puffin puzzle, then gone to Tabletop Time to pick up another—a succulent one of five thousand pieces.

"Are you sure about that one?" Hijiri, the owner, had asked. "The colors can be pretty difficult to match."

"I'll have you know that I've never needed glasses in my life," Loretta said. "Twenty-twenty vision, thank you."

Hijiri held up his hands in mock surrender and wished them luck when they left. Their ambition had grown.

Loretta had asked for Joyce's help filling the window boxes as well, and gardening with Loretta felt pleasantly domestic. It reminded Joyce of gardening with Will at home, and her heart squeezed painfully at the thought of her best friends. She missed them.

They would arrive in town in a few weeks for the wedding, but that was a few weeks too long for Joyce. She called them more often, eager to see their faces and hear the daily news of life in Banff.

And, of course, Joyce had Tori text her every day with updates. No more panic attacks or sudden storms. "I'm fine, Mum," Tori said when Joyce had called her for the third time on one particularly anxious day. "Do I need to start sending you selfies as extra assurance?"

Joyce knew she'd meant it as a joke, but she'd said yes anyway, if only to see her daughter's face more regularly. Burt appeared in the photos a few times as well, and Joyce found herself looking at him more fondly than usual. At least he could look after her daughter when she wasn't there.

～

9 DAYS UNTIL THE WEDDING

The day before Eleanor and Minnie's pre-wedding party at the end of May, Minnie's best friend Dot flew in from Calgary. Joyce went with Eleanor and Minnie to pick her up from the Abbotsford airport. She'd met Dot once over video chat, and she hadn't expected her to be so short. Her husband, Malcolm, had come as well, and he stood a good foot or so taller than the petite woman.

Dot gave them all a hug, including Joyce. "Now I can finally meet the woman bringing my friend's dream to life," she said, squeezing Joyce tightly.

The five of them squished into Minnie's car and drove to Eleanor and Minnie's house. They shared dinner, then sat on the front porch with steaming cups of tea. Malcolm had opted to go for a walk instead, saying he needed to stretch his legs.

Minnie and Dot sat on the right side of the porch in two matching wicker chairs with floral cushions, and Eleanor and Joyce sat on a bench to the left. They'd tilted it slightly, and Dot had pulled up her chair so they made a semi-circle.

"It's not truly tea without this, now, is it?" Dot asked coyly, pulling a silver flask from her sweater pocket. She dumped a splash of whatever was inside—alcohol, presumably—into

Minnie's mug, then her own. Who knew where she'd gotten that from. "Eleanor?" she asked, holding out the flask.

"Oh, go on then," Eleanor said, laughing and taking the flask from her. She poured a dash into her own tea. "Joyce?"

"What is it?" Joyce asked, her eyes narrowed.

"Whiskey," Eleanor said with a wink. "Not the good Scotch kind, I don't think, but still."

Joyce hesitated then held out her mug. She could do with a little kick of warmth.

"Thatta girl," Dot said, and she and Minnie laughed. The two of them had clearly been friends for a long time. They constantly leaned their heads together, chatting and laughing.

"So, how long have you two been friends?" Joyce asked.

Dot tucked the flask into her pocket. "Our whole lives. We both grew up here. We opened our businesses together. I used to own Yellow Brick Books on Main Street, which Leah has been taking good care of for me."

"Oh, wow."

"Dot used to live in that house," Minnie said, gesturing next door.

They'd known each other longer than Joyce had expected. No wonder they acted like two paired puffins.

"I moved to Calgary last summer to be closer to my grandbabies," Dot added.

"It must have been difficult to move away after living here so long." And to move away from Minnie, specifically. It was like Joyce's situation with Will and Andrew.

"Oh, it was," Dot said, blowing out her cheeks. "I thought about it for a long time. But I think we've been managing okay, haven't we, Min?"

Minnie nodded. "It's not easy, but we video call almost every day for tea."

"Including the whiskey?" Joyce asked with a raised brow.

Minnie shot a look at Dot, who smirked. "Including the whiskey."

They quieted for a bit, listening to the low murmur of voices from a nearby backyard. The edges of Joyce's heart felt jagged in her chest as she thought about being separated from her best friends. It was somewhat comforting that Minnie and Dot had recently gone through the same thing and had managed to maintain their relationship, but even so.

Minnie and Dot had started their own quiet conversation about the bookstore, so Joyce turned to Eleanor. She took a deep breath. "Can I ask you something?"

"Hm?" Eleanor looked at her, sipping her tea.

"What was it like to move away from Stonehaven? To move your entire life all the way here?"

Eleanor's gaze shifted over the bright green front lawn. At this time of year, though it was eight o'clock in the evening, the sun still hung boldly in the sky. Joyce had shifted to wearing lighter shirts, not even bringing a cardigan out with her most days.

"Leaving Scotland itself wasn't easy," Eleanor said finally. "I don't think you can ever truly peel yourself away from your home country. And I have a lot of good memories there. Not only of growing up, but with Amara." Her eyes had taken on a faraway look. "I miss things like sitting on the boardwalk, watching the waves crash against the shore. I miss seeing castles everywhere, like centuries of history are at your fingertips." She laughed softly. "And the sheep. There aren't as many sheep here. Even the air has a different quality."

She refocused on Joyce. "But I knew I had to leave. I'd pushed my friends aside after Amara passed . . . You, Will, and Andrew. I wasn't ready to reconnect when I left, and I had this overwhelming sense of guilt that I barely knew Kat. That I hadn't been around for Vera when her husband left. I knew where I needed to be."

"Like an instinct?"

"Yes, you could say that. I felt it in my gut." She pressed a fist to her stomach to illustrate.

Joyce nodded.

Her gut told her to stay with Tori—it was a no-brainer.

And yet she felt unsettled when she thought of leaving Juniper Creek. Her gut was confused.

"Are you thinking of moving here?" Eleanor asked, her voice gentle. "I know you and Loretta have grown close."

Joyce had to clear her throat before she answered. "No. Loretta and I . . . it's just a fling."

Eleanor raised an eyebrow. "It is? I think you've spent more time with her lately than you have with me. I thought there might be something more serious going on."

"No, nothing like that. I enjoy her company"—and many other aspects of her—"but we agreed we'd cut things off after the wedding. Will and Andrew will be moving soon, and I want to be with Tori."

Eleanor must have heard something in Joyce's voice or seen something on her face. She reached over and squeezed Joyce's arm. "Are you alright?"

"Yes, I believe so."

The more she thought about it, though, the less she believed it. Tori pulled on part of her, and Andrew and Will tugged on another. If she was honest, she also gave more of herself to Loretta with each passing day. Withstanding so much love was more painful than it should be. She didn't know how she could scatter her heart and live.

"Have Will and Andrew bought a place yet? Do they have a moving day?"

"Not that I know of." Joyce took a large gulp of tea, hoping the whiskey in it would calm her racing heart. *Buying* a home was so concrete, although she knew it would happen in the near future.

"Maybe you can help them pick a place."

"I'd like that."

Joyce relaxed on the bench, trying to put her worries out of her mind and look on the bright side. Her family would arrive in four days, and she had the pre-wedding party and the wedding itself to look forward to.

And Loretta would be with her for all of it.

CHAPTER TWENTY-THREE

LORETTA

8 DAYS UNTIL THE WEDDING

Loretta picked up Joyce early for the pre-wedding party so they could help Vera and Dot decorate their house and yard. They went around to the backyard, where a circle of chairs already sat, waiting for the guests. A bench stood on the far side, and Kat was in the process of erecting a mint-green backdrop behind it, in theme with the wedding colors. Dot and Vera were arranging a table with a covering that matched.

Vera greeted Loretta and Joyce, then waved them back toward the gate. "You two have handled everything else." She looked at them sternly, her blue eyes a reflection of her mother's. "Let us handle this."

"Are you sure?" Joyce asked, her hands fluttering. Loretta couldn't imagine the restraint it took for her to step aside; she had planned the entire wedding, after all.

"Yes," Dot said, shooing them out. "Go for a walk or something and come back in an hour. We've got this covered."

They stood outside the closed gate for a moment, looking at

each other. "Well," Loretta said, twining her fingers through Joyce's, "I guess we should go for a walk."

Joyce sighed. "We don't have much of a choice, do we?"

They headed for the path around the town pond, which was rather large, but not quite a lake. It wound partially through the trees and along the side of Main Street. If they took their time, they could potentially fill an hour. Or they could sit on one of the benches and look for beavers or birds; it wouldn't be the first time they'd done that together.

The wedding was a mere week away, and Joyce's family would arrive in three days. Loretta had a calendar hanging in her kitchen, and she'd been crossing off each day as it passed, watching Joyce's departure date grow closer.

"Are you looking forward to seeing your family on Monday?" she asked Joyce as they walked.

"I am," Joyce said, perking up. "I was even excited to see Burt, but he has to work now, so he won't be coming. Oh well." She paused. "While Tori and her fathers are in town, I'm going to sleep at the B&B. If that's okay. It would feel odd to stay at yours while they're here."

That made sense and Loretta had expected it, but she wasn't happy about it. "Of course that's okay. You do what you need to do."

They sat on a shaded wooden bench for a few minutes, watching a family of ducks weave through the lily pads as they chatted about the upcoming week and an email Loretta had received about the barn. She had another possible client, and although she'd celebrated when the email arrived, she felt like she was holding her breath until after Minnie and Eleanor's wedding. She needed proof that her venue would be a success.

Loretta put her arm around Joyce, drawing her close. They'd sat in comfortable silence with each other many times, but this silence hung differently.

Joyce's body pressed against hers. Loretta put her arm around Joyce's warm shoulder, the scent of orange blossoms filling her nose as she turned toward Joyce. Joyce was so *real* next to her, solid and present.

But Loretta didn't feel close to her.

Somehow, they sat side by side with a growing space between them, pushing them apart even as Loretta tried to keep them together. Her anxiety was likely playing tricks on her, and she needed to ignore the feeling. Joyce seemed perfectly at ease as she pointed out a turtle suntanning on a log and a woodpecker in a tree across the way.

"Do you mind if we continue walking?" Loretta asked, hoping movement would knock some sense into her. She didn't want doom and gloom overtaking her brain right before a celebration of Minnie and Eleanor's love.

"Not at all." Joyce kissed her cheek, and they began walking once more.

By the time they got back to Vera's house, the decorating was finished. Jamie, the owner of The June Bug and the caterer for the wedding, had taken over the kitchen, whipping up side dishes for a fancy barbeque dinner. Loretta's mouth watered at the corn bread with honey butter, watermelon salad, crispy potato stacks, corn on the cob, and mac and cheese sitting on the kitchen table.

"Can we help?" Joyce asked.

Jamie said yes, and a look of relief spread across Joyce's features. Jamie gave them directions, and Loretta took her place at the counter. Mixing the potato salad helped center her again, taking her mind off her emotions and putting it on the task at hand.

Minnie and Eleanor showed up a few minutes later, exclaiming gleefully over the decor out back. Eleanor looked gorgeous in a long cream dress with a lace overlay, and Minnie wore gray chinos and a pink floral blouse that suited their entire wedding theme perfectly.

Loretta felt underdressed in her sky-blue sundress, but she supposed she wasn't the center of attention, so it didn't matter.

The rest of the guests filtered in over the next fifteen minutes

—all of Minnie and Eleanor's closest friends. Malcolm joined Dot, the two of them striking a conversation with Minnie. Kat's best friend, Charlie, made a grand entrance by setting off a confetti canon and yelling "Congratulations, again!" Dylan and Frankie arrived next, the librarian and her girlfriend, who had taken Minnie and Eleanor's engagement photos and would take the wedding photos as well. Evvie and Matthias slipped into the yard last.

"Sorry, I fell a bit behind making my lemon crinkle cookies," Evvie said, holding out a plate overflowing with the powdered yellow cookies. No one complained, and a few people happily snapped up cookies as an appetizer.

The crowd wasn't huge, but Loretta felt herself withdrawing nonetheless. Even the fact that she knew most of the guests didn't help.

Her go-to strategy at events like this was to latch on to someone she knew well and follow them around like a socially awkward puppy. Otherwise she'd get stuck making small talk and trying not to yawn or come across as overly rude with her one-word answers. She looked for Joyce, but Joyce had found her groove and had weaseled her way into bringing out food dishes and setting the tables, making sure everyone had drinks, and even tucking in Eleanor's tag for her.

Matthias was her next choice. He'd plopped himself into a lawn chair beside Evvie, and luckily an empty one sat on his other side. Loretta made a beeline for it, putting her lemonade in the cupholder to claim her spot.

"Hey." Matthias shifted so he faced forward rather than toward Evvie. "I was wondering where you were. Did you help plan this thing? It's nice." He gestured around them at the market lights on the deck, the gauzy white fabric draped along the fence, the green backdrop with sunflowers along the top, and the tables full of food and drinks.

"Not this time. This was all Dot, Kat, and Vera."

"What do you think we'll be doing? Don't people normally

eat penis cakes or something at these events? Or give each other lingerie?"

Loretta snorted. "That's at bachelorette parties, which Minnie and Eleanor specifically asked *not* to have. I think this will be more chill. Eating, talking, maybe a game or two." The brides had also requested no gifts, so their friends didn't have to sit and watch them open present after present while pretending to be interested—thank goodness. And knowing Minnie, the games would stay on the tame side.

After everyone had eaten their fill of brisket, Loretta's suspicions were confirmed. "Time for a rousing game of charades!" Vera called, and Loretta tried to stifle her groan.

With a sly grin, Joyce made her way through the crowd and linked her arm through Loretta's, pulling Loretta to standing. "Come on, it'll be fun," she said. "We can be on a team."

Even in charades, Joyce was methodical, breaking words into pieces to get Loretta to guess them. In any case, it worked, and Loretta found herself relaxing.

Her relief didn't last long, though.

The next activity was answering a questionnaire about Minnie and Eleanor, and there was a prize for the winners. As she and Joyce worked together to answer the questions, Loretta looked around the yard. Minnie and Eleanor sat side by side, their heads close as they whispered and giggled with each other. Dylan and Frankie sat with their heads bowed together, Dylan shooting exaggerated glares at Evvie and pretending to shield her paper while Evvie stuck her tongue out and Matthias laughed. Everyone was coupled up: Dot and her husband, Kat and Charlie, Vera and Jamie.

They were like one big family, and although Loretta knew that should make her feel welcome, all she could think of was how Joyce would be leaving soon. Then she'd be alone. She'd be the odd one out in this scenario, the one person without a partner to team up with.

"I need water," Loretta said, heading inside to get space. She helped herself to a glass at the sink, then stood looking out the window at everyone. Joyce had scooched over to talk to Vera, and somehow that made Loretta's chest ache even more. She wished her relationship with Joyce wasn't casual.

She wished she could stomach the risk and ask Joyce to be something more. But she couldn't. She couldn't go through that pain again.

After a couple minutes, she returned outside.

"Are you alright?" Joyce asked, grabbing her hand and rubbing her thumb over Loretta's knuckles. "You look a bit peaky."

"I'm fine."

Joyce's brows furrowed, but she got distracted when Kat started a slideshow Vera and Dot had put together. Loretta was thankful. She didn't think she could hide her mood if Joyce prodded her more, and she didn't want to ruin the evening.

The slideshow contained photos from the last few months as well as from Minnie's and Eleanor's pasts. Joyce popped up in a few of them, which she clearly hadn't been expecting because she made a sound of surprise and covered her mouth, her eyes glossy.

While Loretta enjoyed seeing Minnie and Eleanor's journey, it also filled her with a sense of loss, an anticipatory mourning. The feeling got worse when Kat and Charlie presented the brides with a graphic novel they'd made about how Minnie and Eleanor had met. "It's called *Florists Collide*," Kat said, proudly displaying the book. "I did the illustrations, and Charlie wrote the story." Minnie and Eleanor both cried, and Eleanor read the book out loud, making everyone laugh.

Loretta's friends had the perfect romance. They'd started as rivals when Eleanor opened her shop across the street from Minnie's, but over the course of one summer, they'd fallen in love while planning the Sunflower Festival. Minnie had already gone to Scotland to see where Eleanor grew up, and Eleanor had moved in with Minnie not long after. Now they were getting their dream wedding.

Evvie leaned her head against Matthias's arm. "They're so sweet together," she said, cuddling into him. The story had clearly affected Dylan and Frankie too; Dylan grabbed Frankie's hand, and Frankie kissed her on the cheek.

The backyard was turning into a love fest, and Loretta couldn't handle it. She leaned toward Joyce, her voice hushed. "I'm really not feeling well. Do you mind if I head home early?"

Joyce turned to her, eyes full of concern. "Oh no, do you want me to come with you? I can make you ginger tea."

"It's alright. You should be here for Eleanor. Matthias can give you a ride back to the B&B."

"Okay, but I'll call you later." She kissed Loretta's forehead and brushed a curl behind her ear. Loretta closed her eyes, leaning into Joyce's hand. Then she peeled herself away and drove home in a daze.

As much as Loretta wanted to be happy for Minnie and Eleanor—and for the other couples around her—she couldn't help the sinking feeling in her chest. She never thought she'd find love again, but now she had Joyce . . . and their relationship had an end date. It wasn't meant to last.

It wasn't meant to be a true romance.

CHAPTER TWENTY-FOUR

JOYCE

Joyce spent the weekend with Loretta before her family flew in, but Loretta seemed slightly off the whole time—more distant than usual. She insisted that whatever had come over her at the pre-wedding party had passed, but Joyce wasn't so sure.

The two of them went early to Eleanor and Minnie's house on Sunday for their weekly friends' dinner so they could make backup plans in case anything went wrong at the wedding. Even there, Joyce couldn't help but notice how distracted Loretta was.

She sat on a chair instead of with Joyce on the couch, and they didn't share as many casual touches as Joyce had gotten accustomed to. She missed the brush of Loretta's hand on her back, the feel of Loretta's warm palm on her thigh.

Joyce pulled Loretta aside before dinner. "Are you alright? You seem a bit . . . distant. Have I done something wrong?"

"No, no, not at all." Loretta frowned, her arms crossed tightly as if hugging herself for comfort. "I guess I'm just nervous about your family coming tomorrow."

"Oh. Well, I know they'll love you." Joyce closed her mouth before she could add *as much as I do.*

She couldn't say those words out loud. She could barely admit them to herself. One did not *love* someone they had an intentional fling with. The point of a fling was to not get too attached because it wouldn't last. It was supposed to be fun, that was all.

"If you say so."

"I do say so."

Joyce understood Loretta's nerves on some level. Since she hadn't seen Will, Andrew, and Tori in person for so long, her nerves kicked up at the thought of them reuniting. She didn't know if her relationship with Will and Andrew would be the same now that they'd set their moving plans in stone, and she didn't know what her dynamic with Tori would be like either. Lord, she loved her daughter as if she were the sun, but she'd never been away from her for three months before.

Joyce lay awake in bed that night for hours, overcome by the feeling that her life was going to change in some way she didn't expect.

～

5 DAYS UNTIL THE WEDDING

Joyce forewent breakfast the next morning because of her nerves, but she downed two cups of coffee. By the time Loretta picked her up, her jitters were worse.

"It'll be fine," Loretta said, holding Joyce's hand as she drove. "Their plane should land in five minutes or so; I checked. They'll get here safely."

Joyce shot her a smile. "Thank you." She hadn't told Loretta the real reason behind her anxiety—she felt too foolish. She smoothed her skirt and fiddled with her blouse, trying to get her appearance just right as if she was going to an interview. As if these people hadn't seen her walking around in her pajamas with her hair unwashed a million times before.

Although Loretta didn't let on, Joyce knew she was anxious as well. The two of them weren't truly partners, but they cared for each other, and meeting the family of someone you cared for had an air of intimidation. Joyce had been lucky with Matthias; she'd met him a few times now, and he'd been nothing but cordial toward her.

They found a parking spot at the airport, and Loretta put her hand on Joyce's arm. "Want to breathe with me?" she asked softly.

"Please." Joyce closed her eyes and followed Loretta's cues for a minute, inhaling, holding, and exhaling until she could feel her limbs again. When they finally got out of the car, Joyce pulled Loretta into a hug, burying her face in Loretta's lavender-scented curls. "Thank you."

They found the right gate. The passengers hadn't exited yet, even though the plane had landed, and Joyce tried not to tap her foot as she and Loretta waited. The airport wasn't that big, so she'd see her family as soon as they walked out.

People began filtering through the sliding doors, and a familiar face caught Joyce's eye. Before she knew it, she was running into Tori's arms, squeezing her daughter until Tori said, "Mum, I can't breathe." But she was laughing.

Andrew and Will walked up behind her, grins on their faces. All anxiety forgotten, Joyce wrapped her arms around Will's lanky form and pressed her face against his chest. She felt Andrew smush in behind her, the three of them one sandwich of a hug, as always.

Joyce wiped her eyes sheepishly when they disengaged. "It's good to see you," she said, grasping one of Andrew's hands and one of Will's. Andrew's hand was warm and rough, and Will squeezed her fingers as if he never wanted to let go. She took comfort from them both.

"You must be Loretta then," Andrew said, pulling away and holding out a hand to Loretta, who stood a couple steps behind Joyce.

Joyce made the introductions all around, and Will and Tori went in for a hug rather than following Andrew's handshake.

Loretta was all smiles, asking them about their flight as they waited for their luggage. Andrew put everything on a luggage cart, and they filed out to Loretta's car.

"It'll be a squeeze, I'm afraid," Loretta said, but no one seemed to mind.

On the drive back to the Bluebell, Joyce kept turning around, beaming at her family. "Welcome to Juniper Creek," she said, gesturing to the welcome sign like Eleanor had done when she'd first come to town.

An odd sense of pride filled her as they drove down Main Street. She pointed out the shops, adding an anecdote here and there about what she'd bought or seen in them. Unexpected excitement bubbled in her chest, and Loretta smiled at her with amusement in her eyes. Part of Joyce wanted to ask what Loretta was grinning at, but she just accepted it. Accepted that smile and that sparkle, absorbing it and pocketing it to think about later.

Loretta helped them unload their bags at the Bluebell, but she stopped on the doorstep, catching Joyce's hand. "I'll let you settle in. But I'll see you at dinner?"

"Of course." Joyce tried to hide her disappointment that Loretta was leaving, but she supposed it made sense. After a quick look inside to see if her family was watching, Joyce kissed Loretta, putting more passion into it than she usually would. She wanted Loretta to know how much it meant to her that she had met her family.

She didn't stop to think about *why* it mattered that much.

Loretta's eyes widened, but she didn't comment on the kiss.

"Joyce?" Will called from inside.

She waved at Loretta then followed her family up the stairs. Olivia had put Tori in the room next to Joyce's, and Andrew and Will had the room right across the hall. Having everyone together in one space again sent Joyce's heart soaring.

But everything had to come down eventually.

"No naps," Andrew said when they met in the lobby fifteen minutes later. "If we nap, it'll throw off our adjustment to the time zone. We have to stay awake."

"I need a coffee then," Tori said.

"Did someone say coffee?" Dean came over, his hands on his hips and a blue bandanna holding back his long hair. "We've got some in the dining room."

Joyce didn't bother getting herself yet another cup—two was enough for one day. She sat at one of the wooden tables in the dining room instead, watching her family. Tori had braided her hair for the flight rather than putting it in a bun. Andrew and Will wore Crocs, and all three had changed outfits since they arrived.

They joined her at the table. Andrew poured milk in both his coffee and Will's while Will cleaned up a spill, and Tori popped two sugar cubes in hers.

Now that they'd all settled, Joyce wondered if they'd talk about Italy. She knew Will and Andrew had been looking at houses, and she wanted to support them even if it was bittersweet.

Maybe she should have had another coffee after all.

"Much better," Tori said after her first sip of the brew. "This is strong stuff too. I like it."

"So, how are you doing, JoJo?" Will asked, cradling his steaming mug.

"We talked right before your flight," Joyce said, laughing. "You know how I am."

"Well, excuse me for trying to make conversation."

Andrew leaned over and nudged Will good-naturedly with his shoulder.

"I wanted to ask something, actually," she started. "Although if it's too big of a topic, we can save it for another time." Yet another excuse to push it off. She had to stop doing that.

"Oh?" Andrew raised his prominent eyebrows at her as he sipped his coffee. A bluebell on the side of the cup made sure no one could mistake where the coffee had come from.

"Have you talked anymore about . . . Italy?" She forced the name of the country past her lips.

"Oh, we don't have to talk about that right now, do we?" Will said, looking from Joyce to Andrew to Tori and back to Andrew. They had definitely talked more about Italy.

"Are you sure you want to bring this up now, Mum?"

"Well, now I do for sure." Joyce clasped her hands together so tightly that her rings dug into her skin. "Have you made plans?"

"Not quite." Andrew set his cup on the table and rubbed his face, his stubble making a scratchy noise.

"We've been . . . planning for plans," Will said.

What did that bloody mean?

Andrew seemed to have the same thought; he rolled his eyes. "We found a neighborhood we like that's queer friendly, and we've been keeping an eye on house prices. Our realtor found a place she thinks might work, and we've been debating about putting in an offer. We were hoping you'd tell us your thoughts before we went that far, though."

Joyce's body froze up, her eyes glued to the table. They hadn't bought a place yet, but they'd gotten close enough to put in an offer. They had a *realtor* already. This was really happening. They were moving.

She forced herself to swallow, feeling it all the way through her chest as if she'd swallowed a rock. "Can I see photos?"

Will's expression of concern shifted. "Of course! Andy, where's the laptop?"

Five minutes later, Joyce found herself looking at photos of a flat in Lucca, Italy. She had to admit, the photos were gorgeous, and she could easily see Andrew and Will walking around in T-shirts and shorts, eating pasta and going to the beach.

Will couldn't contain his excitement and moved on to show her photos of the archeological remains and the gorgeous buildings in the area. He bounced in his seat like a kid talking about his favorite things. Joyce supposed that's exactly what he was doing.

"So?" Tori asked when Will paused for breath. "What do you think?"

Joyce had zoned out for a second, a photo of a beach and vibrant blue water blurring before her eyes. She blinked at her daughter. "I think Lucca is beautiful. And I think you would be happy there."

A beat of silence rang out over the table.

"The flat has two bedrooms," Will said, "and we could get a sofa bed for more guests. You're always welcome to visit. Tori and Burt too."

"I . . ." Joyce's voice got caught somewhere between her chest and her mouth. "Thank you."

Andrew's expression softened. "I know we've said this before, but it needs to be said again. You know we'd never lock you out, Joyce. You're family. We want you with us whenever you want to be there."

Those words sent a rush of reassurance through her, and tears sprang to her eyes. Before she knew it, she had her face in her hands, tears streaming down her cheeks.

"Oh, JoJo, what's wrong?"

She hiccupped. "N-nothing. I j-just . . ." The words wouldn't come.

Will slid around to her side of the table and enveloped her in a hug. Tori grabbed one of her hands, and Andrew took the other. A little family triangle. "JoJo," Will said, stroking her hair. "You'll always be our third partner, no matter where we go. No matter how far away we are."

Joyce needed to hear those words. She let them settle in her brain then flow through her body, grounding her.

They stayed like that—the four of them connected in one way or another—until Joyce thought she'd explode with love.

CHAPTER TWENTY-FIVE

LORETTA

*L*oretta had told Joyce she'd see her at dinner, but she texted her to cancel, saying she didn't feel well. She wasn't lying; her emotions swirled through her like a maelstrom, making her so nauseous that she'd eaten three ginger chews since she'd gotten home. She kept pulling at her Magen David necklace, the corners of the star leaving red marks on her palm.

When Tori, Andrew, and Will walked through those sliding doors at the airport, Joyce's face had lit up brighter than Loretta had ever seen it. Loretta's heart had ached in that moment, then shame had flooded through her that she could feel anything but happy for Joyce.

Now that rotten thread of shame pulled at her, but her dread at sitting through a dinner with Joyce and her family was stronger. She couldn't sit there and watch them all together, laughing and sharing inside jokes, without feeling like an outsider.

They were her family. Her daughter, her partners. The people she'd built a life with. The people she loved.

Loretta thought maybe Joyce loved her too, but neither of them had expressed as much. And Loretta couldn't dare to hope. She'd failed miserably at keeping distance between herself and Joyce, but it would be easier now with Joyce's family in town.

She had to keep the flame she held for Joyce in check and not allow it to grow any further. She couldn't snuff it—she had to work with Joyce for the wedding still, and she wanted to enjoy what remained of their time together. But she couldn't put her hope in that flame, or it could combust and burn everything down.

~

3 DAYS UNTIL THE WEDDING

Loretta kept up her excuse the next two days, insisting that Joyce stay away so she wouldn't catch whatever Loretta had—even though it was purely emotional. She hoped the space would help her ease off and remember what life was like before she'd met Joyce.

She ate yogurt and stayed in her ratty old housecoat and slippers, her hair a tangled mess on her head. Showering seemed like too much effort, especially when all she did was lie on the couch and mindlessly watch TV.

A knock at the door on Wednesday afternoon made her groan. "Matthias," she called from the couch, "I told you I'm fine! Go away!"

"It's not Matthias!" a voice called back. Joyce.

Loretta sat up so fast her head spun. Joyce wasn't supposed to be there.

"Can I come in, please?"

Loretta bit her lip. She was in no shape to see Joyce right now, not to mention she'd intentionally put distance between them. Now that distance had shrunk to the space between her and the front door.

"Loretta? I'm opening the door."

Loretta opened her mouth to protest, but it was too late. She regretted leaving the door unlocked, but she couldn't do anything about it now.

Joyce stood in the doorway, a grocery bag hanging from one arm and a bottle of ginger ale in the other. "You didn't tell me exactly what was wrong, so I prepared for everything." She took off her shoes then took a good look at Loretta. "Sweetheart, you look terrible."

Squeezing her eyes shut, Loretta sighed. She looked terrible because she *felt* terrible, but not in a physical sense. Joyce being here made it that much worse.

"What can I get for you?" Joyce said, heading over to the kitchen counter. She unloaded her bag. "I have cough drops, cold medicine, Pepto Bismol, anti-nausea pills, Vitamin C drops, zinc, and those ginger chews you like. I also bought packets of that tea mix that's supposed to help with colds."

Pressure built behind Loretta's eyes, so strong it was almost unbearable. Joyce had truly thought of everything, and Loretta wanted to hug her tight and never let go.

"I'd love a ginger chew," she said quietly. She curled up in one corner of the couch beneath her blanket, reaching out a tentative hand to take the ginger chew from Joyce. Their fingers brushed, and Loretta closed her hand tightly around the candy at the thrill that brief touch sent through her.

She was so far gone on this woman.

"Thank you."

Respecting Loretta's unspoken request for space, Joyce sat on the couch across from her. "How are you feeling?"

Loretta shrugged, not trusting herself to answer.

Joyce frowned. "Let me make you tea. The rehearsal is in two days, so you need to rest up and drink lots of fluids."

Unable to stop her, Loretta remained on the couch as Joyce made her tea and oatmeal. While Loretta ate, Joyce told her about how she'd been showing her family around town. "Can I get you anything else?" she asked when Loretta put her spoon in the empty bowl.

"No, thank you. I think I just need a nap."

"Alright. Well, if you need anything, call me, okay? Andrew rented a car. He's waiting outside, actually, so I should probably go. Rest up."

Loretta waved and gave Joyce a small smile, but as soon as Joyce closed the door behind her, she collapsed back into the couch cushions. So much for distancing herself from Joyce.

If anything, Loretta's feelings were even stronger now than they'd been before.

~

ANOTHER KNOCK on the door later that evening sent Loretta into a panic. She was about to fake sleep when she heard Matthias swear as he tripped over the doorframe.

"What's up with you?" he asked once he got inside. "You look like you've seen a ghost." He held up a plastic tub. "Evvie made you cookies."

"I thought you were Joyce." She held her hand out for the container, but even Evvie's cookies didn't appeal to her.

Her brother raised his eyebrows. "You don't want to see Joyce?"

She shook her head. "Not right now."

"Why?" He grabbed a cookie and sat on the far side of the couch, leaning his cane on the table. "What'd she do?"

"She didn't do anything. Well, she came over and brought me stuff." She gestured at the pile of pharmaceuticals still sitting on the counter. "To help me feel better."

"And that's a bad thing why . . . ?"

"Because our relationship is supposed to be *casual*."

"Ah yes. And bringing you stuff to help you feel better is not casual. I suspected there was more going on there." He waggled his eyebrows. "She likes you."

Loretta rolled her eyes. "Of course she likes me, otherwise we wouldn't be in any kind of relationship. But it's going to end in less than a week. I—" She choked on her own words then took a deep breath. "You were right."

Matthias froze with a cookie halfway to his mouth. "I was?"

"Yeah." Loretta sighed. "I'm not meant for casual. But it's too late now."

"Why won't you go see her? Tell her how you feel."

"I can't." She tucked her feet up under her, willing herself not to cry.

"Why?"

She hated when her brother wouldn't let things go.

"Because," she said, "we agreed this would be over after the wedding. I can't go back on my promise. That's why I've been trying to get distance from her this week."

Matthias sighed in exasperation. "Sometimes I don't know what to do with you."

Loretta rolled her eyes. "Nothing. You do nothing. I'm my own person, and I can make my own decisions."

He groaned. "I know, but I think some of your decisions are more self-sabotage than anything." He got up and kissed her on the forehead, softening his words. "But I love you anyway. And you know I'm here if you need me."

"Yeah, yeah. Thanks."

He made her a cup of tea then left to go back to Evvie's—and his place now, Loretta supposed.

To distract herself, she pulled out her sketchbook. But almost every page had a sketch of Joyce on it. Joyce's eyes, her hands as she worked on a puzzle, her hair splayed out over Loretta's pillow. One sketch showed her wearing only Loretta's oversized band T-shirt and underwear, gazing out the window with a cup of steaming coffee in her hands. Loretta stared at the image, wishing she could see Joyce like that every morning for the rest of her life.

But that's not what Joyce was to her.

She slammed the sketchbook shut and groaned, then flopped onto the couch. She rolled until her face pressed into the back cushion. She was a lost cause.

~

1 DAY UNTIL THE WEDDING

Friday morning dawned—the day of the rehearsal dinner. Loretta dragged herself out of bed, fed the girls, and showered, all while giving herself a pep talk. These two days were her chance to shine, to show the barn and the grounds to the guests. She needed to step into her role as business owner and push everything else aside.

She missed Joyce, and she looked forward to seeing her again. Even though she knew that happiness wouldn't last.

After her conversation with Matthias, she could admit that withdrawing for the past week had been self-sabotage more than anything. She thought she'd kicked that habit, but maybe it never went away. Depression was often like that—fighting against yourself and having full awareness that you were causing your own problems but struggling to stop it.

The only solution she'd found over the years was time. Coping mechanisms and medication helped, but time worked the best, even if it moved too slowly.

Now that her brain felt clearer and the fog thinner, Loretta found herself eager to talk to Tori, Andrew, and Will. Loretta would get to know them more, and she'd probably like them. Then she'd feel better about Joyce leaving, knowing that at least Joyce would be happy at her home in Scotland with Tori.

Evvie and Matthias showed up at lunch, then Landon and Gerard came to help set up the chairs outside for the ceremony. The two men may have been construction workers on the surface, but they helped with many of the events around town too, and they were friends with Minnie and Eleanor.

The rehearsal would be outside, then everyone would head into town for dinner at The June Bug. Gerard and Landon would move the chairs into the barn again overnight, where the tables were already set up for the reception the following day.

Loretta had run through the details with all the vendors, and she tried her best to radiate confidence as more people arrived at the farm. Including Joyce and her family.

Joyce wrapped her arms around Loretta, and Loretta held her equally as tightly. She felt so foolish for trying to distance herself for the past week. She could have spent the days with Joyce, but instead she'd locked herself inside. At this point, she wouldn't be surprised if she was as pale as a vampire.

"I missed you," Loretta said softly. She never wanted to let go of Joyce. But in the next second, she had to.

"I missed you too." Joyce pulled away but put her hands on either side of Loretta's face, scrutinizing her. "Are you sure you're alright? You're feeling better today? You don't need a doctor?"

Loretta ran her hands up and down Joyce's forearms. "I'm okay," she said, grinning. "Truly. I feel much better now that you're here."

"Well, isn't that cute." Will joined them on the porch and held his arms open, inviting Loretta into a hug. She accepted the invitation. "Tori and Andrew took the vases to the barn," he said. "But I wanted to say hi first."

With greetings out of the way, Joyce went into wedding planner mode. Loretta had been slightly worried about making small talk, but her fears vanished once Joyce put her to work. She hadn't realized how many tasks were left to do before the wedding party arrived.

Dylan and Frankie showed up next, toting bags of photography equipment. Frankie had a camera around her neck and went straight to the ceremony site to adjust her settings. "I have no idea what most of this is for," Dylan said, setting down a black bag. "I also have no idea how she carried all this shit when she was out in the field." It was no secret that Frankie used to take photos for National Geographic.

Minnie and Eleanor drove in then, with Dot and Malcolm in the back seat. Eleanor wore a flowy yellow dress that fit the rustic summer theme perfectly. Minnie sported a mint-green jumpsuit, likely a cheeky hint at her wedding outfit. When Loretta complimented her on it, she winked.

Once the rest of the guests arrived, they dove into the evening's events.

Even without the full decor, the field where they'd set up for the ceremony looked gorgeous. Wildflowers bloomed farther out where they hadn't trimmed the grass, adding splashes of color to the backdrop. Even with the overcast sky, the scene screamed *spring*, the wooden chairs just worn enough to have charm.

Loretta set Gerard to guard the barn, not wanting anyone to see it until the next day, and he took his job seriously, sitting out front with his arms crossed.

Everyone seemed happy to sit and watch as the wedding party practiced walking down the aisle with Joyce guiding them and giving tips. Frankie snapped photos from angles Loretta wouldn't have even considered. They walked to various songs from the soundtrack of the 2005 *Pride and Prejudice* adaptation, and Loretta found herself tearing up more than once.

"I helped pick the music," Dylan whispered from her spot. Although was it really a whisper if everyone could hear it?

Once they felt comfortable with the procession and they'd talked through the details of the next day, everyone got in their cars to go to the diner. Jamie had left early to prepare—the dinner responsibilities rested on her shoulders, after all.

Joyce walked over, beaming, and linked her arm through Loretta's. "I think that went swimmingly, don't you?"

"I do," Loretta said. All the anxiety and dread she'd felt earlier had evaporated.

"Can I ride with you to the diner?"

"I'd love that." They stood close enough together to brush arms as the remaining guests filtered out, then they got into Loretta's car.

She put on what had become their playlist, and the two of them sang with the windows down. Joyce didn't seem to care that her neat bun became messy, strands of her freshly dyed hair whipping around her face. She must have gotten it touched up earlier that week.

Loretta laughed, her own hair flowing out behind her. She felt free and uninhibited, and if it hadn't been for the music and the wind, she might have told Joyce she loved her right then and there.

But they had to slow down in the line of cars on Main Street, and the mundane task of looking for a parking spot snatched Loretta's courage.

That was probably a good thing.

CHAPTER TWENTY-SIX

JOYCE

The rehearsal had gone well, and satisfaction rolled through Joyce as they entered the diner and took their seats. Jamie had reserved the entire place for the rehearsal dinner, freeing her staff to focus on the wedding party and guests.

Joyce was in the thick of things now. The events would unfold nonstop for the next day and a half, and she embraced every bit of it. They'd been planning this for months, and to see it all play out was exhilarating.

She sat between Loretta and Tori at the long table Jamie had set up between the booths and the kitchen area. It was a bit snug, but everyone fit. Andrew and Will sat across from them, both laughing at something Vera had said.

Eleanor and Minnie had requested carbonara for dinner because it had been one of the first meals they'd shared. And they had apple pie lined up for dessert, which Aaliyah had brought over from the bakery. Joyce remembered Eleanor mentioning that she had brought Minnie apple pie as a peace offering when she first moved to town and opened her shop. Clearly, the baked dessert had worked.

Dinner went well, and Joyce relaxed into the celebratory atmosphere. Will and Andrew asked Loretta about the farm, and

Joyce admired her as she answered. The love Loretta had for her home radiated from her as she told them about it.

Evvie commandeered the entire table so Dylan could share an anecdote about the library. Dylan rolled up her purple-and-blue plaid shirt sleeves and sipped her wine before she dove into the story. It started with Elouise Mitchell coming by the library to complain that the system kept telling her she had an overdue book even though she'd returned it weeks ago.

"So, I asked her how she returned it," Dylan went on. "She said she'd put it in the return bin, as always."

"For context," Frankie interrupted, "the return bin had just been renovated."

Dylan nodded. "We moved it to make things easier for us librarians. Anyway, so Elouise said she put the book there. I had a feeling I knew what had happened, so I asked which bin she'd put it in—the one on the right or the left of the door." She paused, her eyes twinkling. "She'd put it in the left one. Want to guess where our new return bin is?"

"On the right?" Kat asked.

Dylan nodded, smirking. "Elouise had put her book *in the garbage.*"

Laughter broke out around the table. Loretta and Joyce made eye contact, and Loretta's eyes sparkled.

Before people could disperse into smaller conversations again, Joyce stood up and clinked her glass with a spoon. "Hello everyone," she said, doing her best to project her voice down the full length of the table. "Thank you for being here tonight as we prepare to celebrate Eleanor and Minnie's marriage tomorrow."

Everyone cheered, and Minnie's face went red.

"We've got a couple of speeches to kick off the tears, so you can practice your beautiful crying faces." Neither Eleanor nor Minnie knew about these speeches. Joyce and Loretta had planned them as a surprise, and—judging by the looks on her friends' faces—it had worked. "Andrew, would you like to go first?"

"Sure." Andrew pushed his chair back and stood, clearing his throat. Eleanor's face got even brighter, if that was possible, and her eyes glistened. "Most of you don't know me, but I used to be rather close to Eleanor and her late wife, Amara. We've grown apart over the last few years, but I'd like to say a couple things to help make up for that." Andrew talked about when he first met Eleanor—how she and Amara had become an essential part of their friend circle. His tone was bittersweet when he spoke of Amara, but he pulled it all together by welcoming Minnie into the fold. "Amara would want Eleanor to be happy again," he said. "And she'd have been happy to see Eleanor with a woman like you, Minnie."

Minnie and Eleanor both got up to hug him, and Joyce tried to slow her own tears. Amara would be overjoyed for Eleanor; she knew it without a doubt. Sadness and happiness warred with each other in her chest, and she barely held herself together. Loretta put an arm around her, squeezing her close. Joyce sniffed and let Loretta hold her for a second longer, but then she had to announce the next speech.

She sipped her water. "Malcolm, you're up."

"What?" Dot asked, looking astonished. Obviously, her husband hadn't told her what he had planned either. Minnie's eyes widened, and she and Dot made eye contact. Dot shrugged.

"Thanks, Joyce," Malcolm said. "I've known Minnie for a long time." He recounted how he'd gotten to know Minnie more as he fell in love with Dot, how the two of them were a package deal, and how closely they worked together while opening their businesses. "Even before Dot and I got married, Minnie was part of our family." He told a story about how Sydney, their daughter, called Minnie her aunt, and how she had refused to go to kindergarten with her mother. "She always wanted Aunt Minnie to walk with her," he said, smiling fondly. "Now you get to walk with Minnie every day, Eleanor. I hope you know how lucky you are."

Joyce had never seen Minnie cry so much. She gestured to

both Malcolm and Dot, and they joined Minnie and Eleanor for a group hug, all of them crying together.

Moments like this were the highlight of weddings. They made Joyce's heart swell for her own family and friends. For the people she chose to spend her life with. She looked around at them—all but Amara in this room: Will, Andrew, Tori, Eleanor.

Her eyes landed on Loretta. No matter the agreement they made months ago, she didn't want to let Loretta go. She'd never felt this way for anyone before.

Then she looked at Tori, and she knew she couldn't have everything she wanted.

Once everyone had finished their pie, the night wrapped up quickly. They all had a wedding to attend the next day, after all, and some of them were in that wedding.

Will, Andrew, and Tori had parked at the B&B, and they walked there ahead of Joyce, likely to give her time with Loretta.

Loretta wrapped her arms around Joyce's waist, pulling her close. "Tonight was amazing," she said, nuzzling Joyce's nose with her own. "I can't wait to see what tomorrow will be like."

"It'll be even better." Joyce rested her forehead against Loretta's. "I know I said I wouldn't spend the night at the farm with my family here, but I want to go home with you."

"Then do it." Loretta leaned back and tucked a loose strand of hair behind Joyce's ear. "Come home with me. You have to be at the farm early tomorrow anyway."

Loretta's eyes were a darker green in the evening light. Joyce remembered how she'd looked that night at the diner when they'd first met, back when she thought Loretta was quiet and grumpy. They'd come so far since then. "Okay. I'll go grab my things."

Fifteen minutes later, she and Loretta drove back to the farm together, Joyce laughing about her family's expressions when she told them she wouldn't be at the B&B that night.

Later, as they lay in bed at the farmhouse, Loretta's arm draped over Joyce's stomach. Joyce shifted so her nose pressed against Loretta's bare shoulder. Loretta's breathing had slowed; she'd already fallen asleep.

Joyce loved waking up next to this woman. She loved sleeping next to her, listening to her breathing, smelling the lavender all around her. She didn't think she could bear to leave this.

But she couldn't bear to live away from her daughter.

She could barely bear the thought of living away from her best friends.

The last thing she wanted was to fall asleep crying the night before a wedding. And yet, that's exactly what she did.

~

WEDDING DAY

Joyce had no time for emotional reflection the next morning. She and Loretta woke early, and Joyce jumped straight into her morning routine while Loretta fed the girls. They both had large roles to play that day, and neither of them could afford to mess up.

Minnie would get ready at her and Eleanor's house, and Eleanor would get ready at Vera's, then they'd have their first look in private in front of the barn while Frankie recorded it all. The ceremony didn't start until the afternoon, but all the centerpieces needed to be put together, the flowers set in place, the chairs and gazebo decorated . . . Joyce had an entire list of things to accomplish.

Luckily, she had help. She'd hoped to stay close to Loretta as they worked, but the two of them kept being pulled into tasks nowhere near each other.

Before Joyce knew it, guests began trickling in. The area out front filled with cars, and people were forced to park down the lane as well. Good thing they'd set aside a close space for the bridal party to park. They'd set up enough chairs for one hundred and fifty people for the ceremony. Despite Minnie's hope for a small wedding, Joyce had a feeling that wouldn't be enough. It seemed as if the entire town had turned out for the nuptials, regardless of if they'd been invited.

She spotted quite a few faces she recognized from around town: Hijiri and Iris from Tabletop Time, the owners of the Tabby Cat Café, Greg from Mabel's Antiques, Hugo and Gwen from the library, a few of Kat's friends . . . Loretta came over to introduce her to people she didn't know, but there was no way she could remember all their names.

Eleanor showed up before Minnie, and as she stepped out of the car, Joyce gasped. She looked radiant in a ballgown dress with a skirt that resembled layers of white flower petals. The fabric flowed with her as she moved. Her hair was pulled half up and had tiny white flowers woven into it. She looked like a fairy queen.

"You . . ." That's all Joyce got out before she hugged her friend, the two of them laughing breathlessly.

"Thank you," Eleanor said. "Minnie's not here yet?"

"Not yet. Let's get you positioned for the big reveal."

Joyce couldn't stay to watch, but she knew Frankie would show her the video later. She couldn't wait to see the looks on Eleanor's and Minnie's faces when they first saw each other all gussied up.

Loretta already had the music queued, which was perfect. Charlie controlled it, and she gave Joyce a thumbs-up when the ceremony was about to begin.

The procession diverged from tradition, but that fit the wedding. Minnie and Eleanor were both fierce women who did what worked for them and no one else. Joyce signaled Dot and Minnie to walk down together first, then Vera and Kat followed. Eleanor walked down the aisle with Andrew on one arm and Will on the other, and Joyce struggled not to cry as she watched the three of them. So many people held pieces of her heart.

Lorelai, Juniper Creek's mayor and a friend of the brides', stood beneath the flower-covered arch at the front. Her eyes glistened as she smiled, ready to marry two esteemed women.

Joyce finally took a seat next to Loretta and grasped her hand. They had brought this wedding to life together. They'd created something beautiful, and they hadn't even known each other a few months ago.

But it felt like they'd known each other forever, like they knew each other inside and out.

Joyce squeezed Loretta's fingers a hair tighter. She usually floated through wedding ceremonies on a high, but she wanted to feel grounded for this one. To stay present and aware of the people around her, the love covering the entire venue, and Loretta's fingers in hers.

CHAPTER TWENTY-SEVEN

LORETTA

By the end of the ceremony, Loretta had tears running down her face, and most of the other guests did as well. She could tell Minnie and Eleanor's vows came straight from their hearts, and everyone stood to clap and cheer as they walked up the aisle as wives.

Loretta stuck to Joyce's side as the guests each carried their own chair to the barn for the reception. They'd have a break for an hour or so while Frankie took photos of the wedding party, then the show would resume.

As the day's organizers, Joyce and Loretta couldn't exactly enjoy the break. Both stayed in the barn—sitting most of the time, thankfully—delegating volunteers while they completed the floral centerpieces for each table. Somehow, they found a few minutes to escape together to the chicken coop, where they sat on the bench and caught their breaths, watching the hens go about their business.

"This day is amazing," Loretta said. "It's better than I imagined."

"That's because you're a fantastic venue host," Joyce replied.

"I had a good teacher."

They went quiet, enjoying the relative peace in this bubble

away from the chaos of the day. Laughter floated to them from where people played lawn games and chatted over snacks and drinks.

Despite her moment of freedom and courage the night before, Loretta hadn't said anything to Joyce about how she felt. She didn't think it was fair to spring that on her today—or at all now, really. Joyce's flight home was in two days.

Joyce stretched and got to her feet, banishing any chance Loretta had to talk to her anyway. "Time to jump back to it," she said, looking at her watch. "Frankie should be roping the brides back in soon." She kissed Loretta on the forehead, her orange blossom scent enveloping Loretta for a few precious seconds, then she walked to the barn, her pink dress hugging her curves and her matching notebook in hand.

Loretta stood with a sigh and followed her. She'd wanted this —to host weddings, to see the bustle of the guests and the happiness of the couples. But she couldn't imagine running the business without Joyce there to help. It took a lot of energy.

Within the next half hour, the guests were seated and Minnie and Eleanor made their grand entrance as married partners. With most of her responsibilities out of the way, Loretta let loose and leaned into the celebration.

She and Joyce sat together, enjoying the food, the speeches, and the wine. The brides cut the cake, and Joyce grabbed cupcakes for herself and Loretta. "You've got icing on your nose," Loretta told Joyce at one point, laughing as she wiped it off. Joyce stuck out her tongue and wiped icing on Loretta's nose in return.

"Hey! I was *helping* you," Loretta said, pretending to be offended.

"And now I've helped you."

If there hadn't been so many people around, Loretta would have happily chased Joyce with more icing in a small-scale re-creation of their paint fight. But they had roles to play that prevented them from that indulgence.

Minnie and Eleanor had their first dance, gazing at each other as if they were the only people in the room. Loretta's heart pinched. The guests applauded when the song ended, and a few whistles pierced the air. Joyce held out her hand to Loretta, and whether it was the wine, the atmosphere, or her overwhelming emotions, Loretta let Joyce lead her to the dance floor.

"Humor me," Joyce said, wrapping her arms around Loretta's waist. Loretta put her arms around Joyce's neck, and they swayed together to a slow song, their eyes locked. Joyce's blue irises sparkled under the chandeliers, somehow more saturated than usual. Loretta wanted to pull her to the house so they could cuddle on the couch. Just the two of them.

The song ended, but they continued to sway. "Will you come for a walk with me?" Loretta asked. She knew love wasn't a tangible thing. It didn't have a physical form you could touch or see, but she swore it flowed through her veins as she twined her fingers through Joyce's and they emerged into the cool evening air.

The sun had started its descent, the sky blushing pink over the barn but transitioning to an ombre of blue over the house. A few guests had gone outside too, maybe to get space from the noise or heat inside.

Loretta led Joyce to the front porch, and they made themselves comfortable on the wooden swing, holding hands and snuggling. It wasn't the couch, but it would do. They were the only two over here; the new fence had done its job of keeping guests near the barn.

If Loretta was going to say anything, this was the perfect moment to take that leap.

But she thought of her promise that she and Joyce would leave each other on good terms. Telling Joyce she loved her, that she didn't want her to leave, could ruin that promise.

She couldn't do that, so she inhaled and blew out her breath slowly, her heart thudding against her ribs. "Thank you, for all of this," she said instead.

"All of what?" Joyce gripped her hands more tightly, likely hearing in Loretta's tone that what she had to say was important.

"The past couple of months. It's been . . . nice." That was the understatement of Loretta's life.

Joyce's lips parted, her soft sigh mingling with the slight breeze. "Of course. I've enjoyed my time with you too." She turned her head, planting a kiss in front of Loretta's ear.

They sat like that for a while, Loretta pretending they could stay there forever.

CHAPTER TWENTY-EIGHT

JOYCE

They had to move eventually, to return to the reception and make sure the send-off went well. Eleanor and Minnie were off to their minimoon in Tofino the following day. They didn't want a bigger trip since they'd already gone to Scotland that year, and they would be planning the Sunflower Festival in August.

Loretta handed out sparklers to all the guests, and Joyce had everyone make two lines so Eleanor and Minnie could run through the middle. Matthias lit the sparklers at one end, each person lighting the next person's sparkler in a train of glowing sparks that lit up the evening. When everyone was ready, Joyce gave the signal, and Eleanor and Minnie ran hand in hand through the aisle of brightness, smiles taking over their faces. Frankie snapped photos from the end of the lineup, and the crowd cheered.

Across from Loretta, Joyce caught her eye. They grinned at each other.

Once the newlyweds had departed in Minnie's car, the guests started to leave in small groups, the energy of the evening fading. A few people stuck around to stack chairs and clean the barn, and

Tori cornered Joyce as she went to pack up the few remaining cupcakes.

"Mum, you don't have to help with clean up," she said. "There are enough of us to handle this tonight, and we can finish the rest in the morning. Go to bed."

Joyce frowned. "I can't leave until you leave." She looked around for Will and Andrew, and she found them across the barn folding tablecloths. "Isn't Andrew driving?"

"Yes, but I thought you'd spend the night here again. We're leaving in two days."

So you only have two days left with Loretta. Joyce heard the words even though Tori didn't say them.

The thought of spending another night here—possibly her last night here—hurt in a way Joyce had never thought possible, the ache of it settling in her bones.

"Alright. Thank you, my dove." She kissed Tori on the forehead. "I'll see you in the morning."

She said goodnight to Will and Andrew then headed to the farmhouse. The light was on in the kitchen; Loretta must have gone inside already. When Joyce opened the door, Loretta turned her head from where she stood at the counter, making tea.

"Can I have a cup?" Joyce asked.

Loretta seemed relieved, her shoulders relaxing. "Of course. I didn't know if you'd stay tonight."

"I'd like to, if that's okay with you."

"Of course," Loretta repeated. She made Joyce tea, and the two of them sat at the kitchen table under the guise of working on the succulent puzzle that still sat in pieces. Neither of them had the energy to work on it, but neither of them moved to go to bed either.

Matthias knocked on the door around eleven to tell them everyone had gone home for the night. "I'm surprised you're both still awake," he said.

"We've got a puzzle to finish." Loretta gestured at the mess of pieces in front of them. They'd started organizing them by color in small paper plates, but the puzzle looked sad with only the border finished and a few pieces put together here and there.

"Good luck with that." He gave them a wave then left.

"We can't finish this," Joyce said, trying to sound lighthearted. Even if they spent every waking moment on it before Joyce left, it wouldn't be done.

Loretta sighed. "I know. Let's go to bed." She held out a hand to Joyce, and Joyce took it, following Loretta to her bedroom.

They held each other close that night—closer than usual. Joyce wanted to stay awake, to breathe in Loretta's springtime scent and memorize the lines of her face, but her eyelids drooped and she drifted off before she could count to thirty.

CHAPTER TWENTY-NINE

LORETTA

The next day, Loretta watched Joyce bustle around the barn, packing away the table linens. It was their last full day together, and Loretta wanted to draw out every moment.

Many of the wedding guests returned to help clean the farm, and with their help, everything looked as good as new by lunchtime. Jamie brought sandwiches and snacks from the diner for lunch, and they sat around on the porch and on picnic blankets in Loretta's front yard while they ate.

"I'll send you a few photos to use for your website and social media," Frankie said. She and Kat sat on the porch steps with Loretta, Joyce, Dylan, Evvie, and Matthias as they talked about how well the wedding had gone. "I think people will love it."

"They already do," Loretta said, her mood lifting. "I've already had two requests to see the farm, and someone else emailed me yesterday inquiring about shooting a music video here." She wasn't sure what had happened to attract people to her website, but she was grateful for it.

"A music video?" Kat said around a mouthful. "That's so cool! Did the logo work out?"

Loretta nodded and pulled up the venue website on her phone to show Kat. When she handed the phone over, she noticed Joyce watching her with an expression of pride. Loretta was going to miss that face.

When they finished eating, Joyce slid closer to where Loretta sat on the top step. "How are you feeling?" she asked.

Loretta could have answered that question in so many ways, but she knew Joyce was referring to how she felt in that moment with all the people over. Just that morning, they'd talked about how exhausting weddings could be, even though they both loved them.

"Tired. I think I'll need at least two weeks to recover." She was joking, but barely.

Joyce nodded and got up. She whispered something to Matthias, and the two of them started ushering people home. Loretta stayed on the porch stairs, waving and calling her thanks to everyone for helping.

Finally, only Joyce and her family were left. Joyce said something to Tori that Loretta couldn't hear, and Tori nodded. She stayed sitting on the blue-and-white plaid blanket with her fathers as Joyce returned to the porch.

"Shall we visit the goddesses?" she asked.

It was an odd request, but Joyce seemed to have an agenda, so Loretta let Joyce pull her to her feet. They headed around back and sat once more on the bench across from the chicken enclosure.

Loretta put her arm around Joyce, and Joyce leaned against her shoulder. "So," Joyce started.

" . . . so?"

"I fly home tomorrow."

"I know." Loretta had cried so much yesterday, she had no interest in crying more today. The last thing she needed for the rest of the day was a headache.

"Will you come to the airport to say goodbye?"

She had thought about this already, and she didn't want to. She didn't want to see Joyce walk through security and out of her life, but she knew it was important.

"Yes," she said, her voice quiet. "I'll be there."

Joyce's face relaxed. "Perfect. I'll see you tomorrow then?"

Loretta held Joyce tighter, and the two of them sat there in a silence rife with meaning until Will came around the corner of the house.

"Sorry to interrupt, but we said we'd go to Vera's for tea this afternoon." He looked at his watch. "We said we'd be there ten minutes ago."

Joyce straightened, and Loretta reluctantly pulled her arm away. "Right. Okay," Joyce said.

She twined her fingers with Loretta's as they went back to the front of the house. Loretta clung to her, not wanting to let go.

But she had to. She knew she had to.

This wasn't even the real goodbye. Not yet.

"Thank you for your help," she said as she hugged Tori, Will, and Andrew.

"Of course," Andrew said. Will gave her a look as if he knew how much pain she currently felt.

The three of them headed for the car, giving Loretta and Joyce a moment alone. Andrew had taken Joyce's overnight bag already, so she had nothing left to carry.

Loretta and Joyce hugged, holding each other tightly. Loretta somehow managed to let go when Joyce pulled away to go to the car. She stayed outside and waved as they drove off, watching the car grow smaller until it turned onto the highway.

Then she walked inside, feeling numb. As soon as she closed the door, it crashed into her: Joyce was leaving tomorrow. Loretta probably wouldn't see her again after that. They'd had something good for a few months, and now that was over.

She sank to the ground, pulling her cardigan tighter around herself. She burst into tears, her chest heaving, tremendous waves of helplessness washing over her.

So much for not crying.

CHAPTER THIRTY

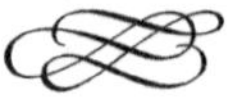

JOYCE

*J*oyce thought she'd be happy to go home. She missed Banff terribly, even the rain and the cold. She missed her own bed, her puzzle table, and even their dishwasher that never properly washed the dishes.

But saying goodbye to Kat, Vera, and Loretta at the airport was agonizing. She'd just gotten close to Eleanor and her family again.

And Loretta . . . Joyce hadn't anticipated leaving her to feel like tearing out a piece of her heart. Flings weren't supposed to end like this. For the first time, Joyce didn't feel sated after a short-term relationship.

"I'm going to miss you," Joyce said to Loretta, tears in her eyes. "If you ever want to talk . . . you know where to find me."

Loretta didn't speak. She simply nodded and kissed Joyce gently.

She smiled and waved with the others as Joyce walked with Tori, Andrew, and Will through security. And that was it.

They were on their way back to Scotland, and Joyce could put Juniper Creek behind her.

But for the entire flight to Glasgow, all she could think about was Loretta. She'd been so composed when Joyce left, which Joyce hadn't expected. Maybe she'd resigned herself to their parting more than Joyce had. Maybe she'd be fine again on her own with her business to keep her busy.

Joyce didn't think she'd get over Loretta as easily, regardless of how short-term she'd intended their relationship to be. She never thought she'd find love like that . . . She could admit to herself now that what she felt for Loretta *was* love. A love more serious than any she'd found before, a love that showed her she could embrace change and branch out on her own.

She realized now that she'd never been interested in a long-term relationship because she'd never felt strongly enough about anyone to want them in her life for longer than a month or two. Her world had revolved around her family, and she hadn't felt the need for anything else. But now that everything was shifting, now that everyone was going their own way . . . Loretta had reminded Joyce of who she was on her own. Of what she wanted for herself.

Images of her time with Loretta flitted through Joyce's mind. Loretta sketching her in the barn, primer smeared on her clothes. Loretta sitting on the bed at The Marigold, her hair damp. Loretta bringing her cake, giving her a puzzle, dancing with her to glam rock.

Loretta made her feel fundamentally *herself.*

She'd never told Loretta how she truly felt, but that was probably for the best. Now she had to figure out how to get through heartbreak—a heartbreak made even worse by the fact that they hadn't hurt each other.

They'd kept their promise—they'd left each other on good terms. But it didn't feel good.

Tori tried to get Joyce to watch movies with her on the flight, but every few seconds, something in the films reminded Joyce of Loretta. The way someone spoke, the sweater a character wore, a farmhouse passing in the background, someone using the word *chutzpah.*

Tori leaned her head on Joyce's shoulder to try for a nap, and all of Joyce's reasons for flying back to Scotland washed over her. But she no longer felt certain that she'd made the right choice.

She didn't know how she could go back to her old life. Back to who she was before.

She didn't know if going *back* was what she truly wanted.

~

THE PAIN of losing Loretta didn't dim over the next few weeks. If anything, it grew worse as Will and Andrew bought the house in Italy. There was no hiding it now, no matter how hard Joyce tried. They were leaving. They had a moving date and everything, and years' worth of knickknacks and belongings disappeared from around the house as they packed.

To keep herself occupied, Joyce went out on the *Guillemot Guide* with Tori as she gave her wildlife tours. They'd found a new skipper—a hardy woman named Greta—and Will had shown her the ropes. Tori ran the company on her own now, and Joyce had to admit she did a bang-up job of it.

"Mum, are you sure you want to come with us again?" Tori asked on the fifth day in a row with Joyce at her side.

"I'm sure." Joyce zipped up her jacket and followed Tori onto the boat, waiting for the guests to arrive.

The more time she spent with Tori on board—with Tori *in charge*—the more confident she felt in her daughter's abilities. Tori didn't show any hint of fear, even after her most recent storm scare. She moved around the boat like she'd been born at sea, and even on a day with rougher waves, she didn't even flinch.

That afternoon, as Joyce listened to Tori explain the gannet colony to a group of bird watchers, she realized she wasn't overly worried about Tori anymore. She didn't watch her constantly to see if she was okay. She could turn her back and look out across the vastness of the sea without worrying that her daughter needed her.

And every time Joyce looked out across the water, she thought of Loretta. Loretta would love the sea and all the birds.

At the end of the tour, after the guests had disembarked, Tori approached where Joyce stood at the rail and put an arm around her. "You alright?"

"Hmm?"

"You seem distracted today. You didn't even laugh when that bloke got pooped on."

"Oh. I'm just thinking."

"About?"

Joyce leaned her head on her daughter's shoulder. "This and that."

Tori made a thoughtful noise. "Does *this and that* have dark curly hair and live on a farm in Canada?"

A bittersweet smile crept over Joyce's face. "Maybe."

She hadn't talked to Loretta since she'd left. She could have reached out, but trying to be long-distance friends would likely increase Joyce's pain. Loretta hadn't tried to break the silence either.

"Mum."

Joyce turned to look at her daughter. Tori's hair was wild around her face, her cheeks tinged red from the wind. "Yes, my dove?"

"I don't understand why you came back with me."

The statement was so matter-of-fact, it took Joyce aback. "What do you mean?"

"I mean, you knew Da and Dad were moving. Why didn't you stay with Loretta? I saw how you looked at her at the wedding. You moved around each other like you lived in each other's orbits or something. Even Burt and I don't do that."

Had they been like that? "It wasn't . . . We agreed we would split up after the wedding, and that's what we did. It was just a fling."

"Bollocks. You miss her. I know you do. What's keeping you

here? If it's me, you better buy a plane ticket right now and get back there."

If it hadn't been for Tori's tone, that comment would have hurt. In fact, it still hurt, even though Joyce knew how Tori had meant it.

"I have every right to stay with my daughter. With your fathers leaving . . ." She took a deep breath. "I can't lose my whole family at once."

"Mum." Tori grabbed Joyce's shoulders and pulled her into a hug. Joyce had to turn her face so she could breathe, but she held her daughter tightly anyway. "Remember what Da and Dad said at the B&B in Juniper Creek? You won't lose us no matter where we are. No matter where *you* are. We're family."

"I know," Joyce whispered. "I do know that." And she did. She thought back to her three months in Canada, to how often she'd talked to her family over phone or video call. It hadn't been the same as talking in person, of course, but they'd all made the effort to be part of each other's lives as much as possible. They hadn't lost each other, and they wouldn't in the future either.

Tori leaned back and wiped a tear from Joyce's cheek. "And I'm okay. I've been okay for a while now, even if I need to call you to talk sometimes. I know you worry about me, but you don't worry any less here than you would if you had stayed with Loretta. And I don't like the idea that you turned down a relationship with her just to be with me. I want you to be happy, Mum. You've given our family so much, and now you've found someone who lights you up like I've rarely seen before. Don't let that go."

Joyce's bottom lip trembled as Tori's words sunk in. "I'll think about it," she said.

Tori nodded. "Let's go get a cuppa."

CHAPTER THIRTY-ONE

LORETTA

*I*f Loretta hadn't had her new business, she would have fallen into a serious funk when Joyce left. Even with the growing interest in the farm, Loretta struggled to get out of bed most days. She had a lot to be thankful for, and she felt better whenever she got up and went outside, but sometimes everything that had happened overwhelmed her.

Joyce had been gone for a month. Loretta had booked two more weddings and the music video shoot, but nothing brought her joy like she wanted it to. When she'd started the business, she'd put her whole self into it. She'd felt like creating this venue gave her renewed purpose. But that seemed to have faded away.

She still looked forward to hosting the weddings, of course. But she moved around as if wading through a gray cloud, like everything around her had dimmed. Sometimes she felt so close to the edge of the cloud, like if she could take one step out of it, she'd be okay again. But she couldn't figure out how.

As always, her hens gave her the most motivation. She started carrying Persephone around with her more than usual to remind herself she had living beings relying on her. Even if she didn't feel like existing for herself, she had a responsibility to others.

Matthias and Evvie started coming over almost daily without

comment. They must have noticed her change in demeanor, and she appreciated them even if their presence also annoyed her.

"Can we please put away this puzzle?" Matthias asked one day as he stood at the counter mixing pancake batter for brunch.

The succulent puzzle Loretta and Joyce had been working on still lay sprawled on the kitchen table. Loretta hadn't worked on it since Joyce left, but she hadn't had the heart to box it up. It sat there, reminding her of what she'd lost every time she walked into the kitchen.

"It's not finished," Loretta said.

"But you're not working on it," Matthias replied gently. He knew what it meant to her, but he also wasn't wrong in his request. Why leave it out if she wasn't going to finish it? She couldn't leave it there forever.

Evvie looked up from the couch where she was knitting. "What if I worked on it with you?"

Loretta bit her lip. "I appreciate that, but . . ." But it was the puzzle she did with Joyce. They were supposed to finish it together. "Maybe we should just pack it up." Without thinking too hard about what she was doing, she swiped all the pieces and the paper plates into the puzzle box that still sat on one of the kitchen chairs.

Neither Matthias nor Evvie said anything, but Loretta saw the concerned glances they exchanged.

It's only a puzzle. Loretta went to her room and opened her closet. She stood there for a moment, staring at the cardboard box full of her mementos of her relationship with Gail. She put the puzzle on top and tried to ignore the lurch in her chest as she closed the closet door.

When she returned to the kitchen, Matthias had set up the table for brunch. A plate piled high with pancakes sat surrounded by bowls of fresh fruit, a bottle of pure maple syrup, and a bowl of whipped cream.

The meal should have been delicious, but food hadn't appealed to Loretta for weeks now. She ate because she had to, and she made herself take seconds so Matthias wouldn't comment on her lack of appetite. No one spoke much as they shared the meal, and Loretta couldn't help but think the somber atmosphere was her fault.

After brunch, the three of them cleaned up together then Loretta slid on her worn sneakers. "I'm going to sit outside for a bit," she said. She didn't want to keep dragging others down with her.

But as soon as she sat on the bench next to the chicken enclosure, the back door opened again and Matthias walked out. "Do you mind if I join you?" he asked.

Loretta gestured to the seat beside her. Matthias sat and inhaled deeply, a smile on his face. "Sometimes I wish I could sprawl in the sun like that," he said, looking at the hens. "If I had feathers to ruffle, I would do that too. Being a hen seems so easy."

"Until a fox comes along," Loretta said wryly.

"Well, sure. But if my caretaker was as anal as you are, I wouldn't have to worry about that."

They sat in companionable silence for a few minutes, listening to the sounds of summer and letting the breeze caress their skin.

"Can I ask you something?" Matthias said eventually. He tapped his cane on the ground a few times, pushing around the loose dirt.

"Sure."

"Why haven't you stayed in touch with Joyce?"

Loretta frowned. She hadn't been expecting that question; she didn't think she'd told him about her lack of communication with Joyce.

Matthias seemed to read her mind. "I know you. You've been unhappy since she went home, and you left that puzzle out for so long without touching it. Evvie's worried about you."

Loretta knew her brother. Matthias was worried too, even if he wouldn't outright say it.

"I'm fine," she said, looking at her shoes. "I've had depression for years. I know I'll get over it." These episodes were always temporary, like clouds passing through. They never felt like it, though, and Loretta had to remind herself daily that her emotions would change. She just had to hang on until they did.

"I know, I know. But I wonder if this is different than usual."

Loretta loved her brother, but she didn't love people psycho-analyzing her. She tried not to get her hackles up as she asked, "What do you mean?"

"I mean, I think you're grieving. I think you miss Joyce and what you had with her." Matthias paused. "Do you remember how Dad used to call you the queen of kvetching?"

Loretta huffed out a laugh. "Yeah." He'd always said it endearingly, even if kvetching wasn't an endearing thing to do.

"You didn't complain much at all when you were with Joyce. About anything. You were happier than I'd seen you in years."

Loretta bit her lip.

"Am I wrong?" Matthias asked.

Everything she hadn't let herself feel bubbled up in her chest, and suddenly she gasped as if she hadn't truly taken a breath for ages. Matthias put his hand on her back, the weight and warmth of it reassuring as she counted her breaths and calmed herself down.

"No," she said finally. "You're not wrong." And then it all came out. "I didn't want her to leave, but we'd agreed that what we had was temporary. It wasn't meant to last, for either of us. I thought that would be a good thing for me, that I wouldn't risk getting hurt like I had with Gail, but . . . I fell in love with Joyce. I wish I hadn't, but I did. And I don't know what to do about it now. I didn't think . . . I thought Gail had been it for me. That I wouldn't find anyone else after her. I didn't really want to, either, after how we broke up.

"But Joyce was different. She made me want to be better and do more. She's so full of life, and she knows what she wants. Even with my business . . . I think I spent so much time with Joyce setting the whole thing up that it doesn't feel right to host weddings without her. Sure, this is *my* business, but she helped me make it."

Joyce had brought her out of her shell again. Made her want to truly *live*.

"Would you mind if I shared my opinion?" Matthias asked.

Loretta laughed. "You're going to share it even if I say no."

He shrugged. "You and Joyce probably had good reasons for agreeing to a short-term relationship. But I saw how you were together at the wedding, and I think you felt more for each other than you bargained for. In fact, I know *you* did. It's not my place to make this decision for you, but I think you should reach out to her and see what she says. You never know."

Mathias sounded as if he was talking from experience, and he likely was considering how he and Evvie had gotten together. Loretta didn't know the details, but she knew Evvie had been hurt somehow and Matthias had put himself out there to get her back. Even though he'd been hiding his identity, he came forward and sang a song he dedicated to Evvie in front a huge crowd of people on New Year's. Loretta's heart tingled. He'd been so brave. Why couldn't she be the same?

"What if I ask her and she doesn't feel the same way?" Loretta asked. "Wouldn't I save myself the hurt if I don't say anything?"

"If you don't ask, you're not even giving it a chance," Matthias said. "Do you regret being with her?"

"Of course not. I don't regret a single second."

"Then you have nothing to lose, do you? Even if she says no, you'll still have those months with her. It's worth the risk, Etta. Love is always worth the risk."

That struck a chord. "I think . . . I need to take a walk."

"Go for it."

Loretta got up and followed the fence along the farm, her sneaker laces getting caught in the tall grass. Her mind raced. She and Joyce had agreed to a short-term relationship, but maybe that didn't need to be set in stone. Loretta hadn't even considered discussing it. She'd thought that if Joyce felt something more, she'd say something, but maybe she wouldn't have. Loretta hadn't, and she'd definitely fallen harder than she'd intended.

When she got back to the farmhouse, she found a sticky note on the table with Matthias's handwriting: *Gone to run errands. Be back for dinner.*

Loretta made herself a cup of tea and sat on the couch, still thinking. Her gaze landed on her sketchbook. She flipped it open, looking over each drawing of Joyce and letting herself truly feel the love she'd been suppressing.

Joyce had brought light into her life again. She'd given Loretta back her confidence in herself and shown her that she was worthy of love.

Matthias was right. Love was always worth the risk. Loretta had given up hope before she'd even really tried to make things work with Joyce.

She had to know if Joyce felt the same way about her.

Loretta grabbed her set of charcoal pencils and flipped to a fresh page in her sketchbook. Determination moved her pencil along the page. The portrait came to life in pieces, and Loretta didn't stop to look at the whole until she'd finished.

With newfound hope flowing through her veins, Loretta penned a letter to go with the portrait. She'd send them both the following day. She could call Joyce instead, of course, but this felt more meaningful.

She hoped Joyce would like it.

CHAPTER THIRTY-TWO

JOYCE

Since Joyce could no longer avoid the fact that Will and Andrew were moving, she decided to help them pack. Their flight would leave the following Monday, and that would be that. They'd be gone.

"What about this one?" Will asked, turning around so Joyce could see the blue cable knit sweater he wore from all angles. She sat on his and Andrew's bed, helping him figure out which clothes to take with him and which ones to donate. Andrew had simply gotten rid of anything he hadn't worn in the past month, but Will was more sentimental than that.

"It looks nice, but I doubt you'll need a sweater that thick in Italy," Joyce said.

Will sighed. "You're right, I suppose. I really like this one, though." He went to put it in the donations box but stopped. "What if you keep it here for me for when I visit?"

"Are you planning to visit much? I thought the idea is that Tori and I would travel to visit you instead."

With a groan, Will dropped the sweater into the box. "Why must you be so logical? You've been spending too much time with Andrew."

Joyce laughed. She'd miss days like this.

They both turned at a knock at the door. "Hiya," Tori said, leaning against the doorframe. "Just grabbed the post. There's a package for you, Mum." Her eyes sparkled, and Joyce frowned. What type of package would put that expression on her daughter's face?

She met Tori at the door, and Tori handed her a cardboard tube, the type used to transport posters and paintings. Joyce took it from her, looking for the shipping label.

She inhaled sharply when she saw who it was from.

Will peered over her shoulder. "Oh. Maybe you should sit before you open it." She let him steer her back over to the bed. "Do you want us to leave you alone for a while?"

"No, please stay," she said, grasping his hand. He sat on one side of her, and Tori sat on the other.

"Well, here goes." Joyce used her nail to cut through the tape on one end of the tube, then she took a deep breath and slid out the contents: one large role of thick paper, and one much smaller. Carefully, she unrolled the larger one first, and her breath caught in her throat. "Oh."

"Oh my," Will said. "That's beautiful." He took it from her, holding it open so the three of them could see it better.

It was a portrait of Loretta and Joyce looking at each other, affection clear on both their faces. Loretta hadn't added much detail to the background, but the way she'd shaded their foreheads and cheeks made Joyce think she'd pictured them standing in the barn beneath one of the chandeliers.

"It's unfair that she can draw herself that well," Joyce said, laughing shakily. She traced the lines of Loretta's face. "This whole thing is unfair."

"Open the letter," Tori said softly, handing her the other paper, which she must have dropped.

Joyce's hands trembled as she did so.

Joyce,

I should have told you this before you left. I know we agreed to have a fling, but I overshot my mark. I fell for you, and it aches to be apart from you. I miss you dearly. I don't know how we can make it work, but I know we can, if you want us to be together as much as I do. May I visit you in Scotland? I want you to show me the puffins.

Yours,
Loretta

THE LETTER WAS SHORT, but it said everything it needed to.

"JoJo?" Will said, nudging her lightly. "How do you feel?" She couldn't tell if he'd read the letter over her shoulder, but he clearly got the gist of the message.

Tori slid the letter out of her hand and looked it over.

"I . . . I think I agree with her," Joyce said.

When Tori looked at Joyce again, she had tears in her eyes and a smile on her face. "I agree with her too. Are you going to invite her to visit?"

Joyce blew out a breath. She'd felt a decision brewing within her for days, and this letter was the nudge she'd needed. Her mind swirled with thoughts of the Sunflower Festival coming up in August, the one where Minnie and Eleanor had solidified their relationship a year prior—the one they'd based their wedding decor on.

"No. I want to do something else." Joyce grabbed one of Tori's hands and one of Will's, looking at each of them in turn. "Let's get Andrew. We need to have a family meeting."

CHAPTER THIRTY-THREE

LORETTA

*L*oretta had sent the letter and the portrait a month ago, and she hadn't received a response. No letter, no phone call, no email. She'd even asked Eleanor and Minnie if they'd heard anything from Joyce, but they hadn't. Not about her, anyway.

Maybe she could have convinced herself that the package got lost in the mail, which happened more often than people thought. Except she'd paid for tracking, and she knew the package had arrived weeks ago.

That could only mean one thing: Joyce didn't want her to visit. She didn't want them to be together. She didn't want to see Loretta again.

It hurt—of course it did. But somehow, she was at peace even with the knowledge that Joyce didn't want to be with her. At least now she didn't have to wonder what would happen. She'd reached out and laid herself bare in front of Joyce, and she'd received her answer.

They'd had a wonderful time together, but Loretta needed to move on with her life.

She knew now it was possible to feel love and joy again, that the risk was worth it even if those feelings didn't last. She could still feel them, and she valued herself enough to allow herself to feel them again.

She'd likely pine for Joyce for a while, but there was no possibility of a reunion unless she forced it, and she'd never do that to Joyce. She had to walk forward and not look back.

So when Evvie invited her to go to the Sunflower Festival that weekend, Loretta said yes.

EARLY SUNDAY AFTERNOON, Loretta drove with Evvie and Matthias to the park by the pond along Main Street where the town held most of its big events. Loretta wouldn't usually agree to help set up for something like this—the event itself would be exhausting enough with all the people—but she wanted to put herself out in the world once more.

"There you are!" Eleanor greeted them as she walked over from a nearby booth, giving all three of them a hug. Her wedding ring caught the sunlight and sparkled on her finger.

"What can we help with?" Matthias asked.

She directed him and Evvie to help with the sunflower garlands on a few of the kiosks. "And Loretta, could you help with the sunflower jars?"

"Sure, sure." She followed Eleanor over to one of the tables where Minnie, Kat, and Dylan sat putting sunflowers into mason jars.

"Last year we had too many flowers, and this year I don't know if we got enough," Minnie said, covering her mouth in concern.

Eleanor leaned over to kiss her forehead. "It'll be fine, darling. If we don't have enough, we'll steal some from the barrels and add more greenery."

Seeming appeased, Minnie nodded and cut the stems off a few more flowers before handing them to Kat.

Loretta was put on burlap duty, fixing any ribbons that had

fallen off the jars from last year's event. The town didn't have a huge budget for festivals, so they reused decor whenever they could, and it got beat up quickly. She got into the groove, focusing on her work, and she was almost disappointed when Lorelai came over and told them to go home.

"There's nothing left to do except wait for the festival to start in a few hours," she said, looking at her phone. "Speaking of, I need a nap if I'm going to get through the rest of today." She waved then joined the other volunteers heading to the cars for a break before the festival began that evening.

"Why don't you come to our place this afternoon?" Eleanor asked Loretta. "We're having tea with Dot over video call, and we have snacks."

More peopling was not Loretta's idea of relaxing, but Matthias and Evvie wanted to go, and she reminded herself that she was worth putting in the extra effort. She had to risk some discomfort to keep up her relationships. To make the life she wanted to live. So she said yes.

The group of them walked over to Minnie and Eleanor's house, and Eleanor made them tea. Evvie decided to whip up a batch of cookies and Loretta helped her, taking comfort in the feeling of the dough beneath her hands as she rolled it into balls.

Visiting made time pass quicker, and before she knew it, they were walking back to the festival grounds.

Loretta had to admit, the festival looked magical like it did every year. Strolling under the trees full of fairy lights made her feel lighter than she had since Joyce left. It pulled her slightly out of the cloud she'd been in, letting her see glimpses of the world in clarity again.

She breathed in the smell of fresh popcorn and corndogs, and her stomach rumbled in response. Matthias, who walked ahead of her, hand in hand with Evvie, laughed. "I heard that from here," he said. "I guess our first stop will be for food."

Loretta rolled her eyes but didn't complain when they went

straight to a kiosk to grab corndogs, then headed over to the tables in front of the gazebo.

The grounds were full, as they always were for the summer festival, families wandering around and guests lining up at the food stalls. A few kids showed off their cartwheel skills on the grass while a group of teenagers ran through the haybale maze, tripping over themselves and laughing.

"Snow cones after the opening speech?" Minnie asked Eleanor.

Eleanor smiled, and the love in her gaze as she looked at Minnie tore at Loretta's heart. "Of course."

"Me too!" Kat said. "I'm the original snow cone buddy."

"Obviously," Minnie replied.

Despite the joyful atmosphere, Loretta felt a bit out of place. Once again, she found herself at a table full of couples—except for Kat, but Kat had their best friend, Charlie. Loretta had all these people, of course, but it wasn't the same as being with that one person who knew you so well they could practically read your mind.

Her thoughts flitted to Joyce, and she refocused her attention on the gazebo where Lorelai stood, waiting to start the opening speech. Joyce had gone, and she wasn't coming back. If Loretta told herself that enough times, maybe it would stop hurting.

"Welcome to this year's Sunflower Festival!" Lorelai said into the microphone, and everyone cheered. "This festival takes place on the traditional and unceded ancestral lands of the Stó:lō Peoples, also known as the People of the River, particularly the Semá:th and Máthxwi First Nations. As you enjoy the festivities, please take a few minutes to visit our information booth to learn more about the history of the Fraser Valley and the Peoples who have lived here since time immemorial. If you can, please also donate to one of the societies to help provide resources and space for connection and reconciliation. Thank you, and enjoy the evening!"

After the cheering died down, Loretta got up to make her

donation. When she went back to the table, Eleanor asked, "Would you like to get snow cones with us?"

"I'm not much of a snow cone person, but thanks."

"The kettle corn stall is right next to it," Eleanor said. "What about that?"

Loretta sighed. She got the feeling Eleanor was trying to get her more involved, and she appreciated it even though she was slightly annoyed. "Okay, fine. Matthias? You wanna come?"

Her brother shook his head. "Nah, I'm good here." Something about his expression made her suspicious, but she couldn't figure out exactly what it was.

"You sure?"

"Yeah, yeah, I gotta hold the seat for Evvie. She's gone to get her face painted." He gestured with his chin, and sure enough, Evvie sat at the face painting booth, half a rainbow glittering on her cheek as the painter worked on the rest.

Loretta shrugged and followed Minnie, Eleanor, and Kat across the grounds to the snow cone booth. "I'll go grab my popcorn," she told them.

Eleanor reached out as if to stop her, but her eyes locked on something over Loretta's shoulder, and she straightened again and smiled. "Alright. Yes, go get your popcorn."

What was going on with people tonight?

Brushing off Eleanor's strange behavior, Loretta turned toward the kettle corn stall.

And walked straight into Joyce.

She backed up, holding her breath and doing a doubletake. Joyce stood in front of her, holding a bouquet of flowers and looking sheepish. She wore a pink sundress, her hair pulled back in its usual low bun.

"Hi," she said.

Loretta stood rooted in place with her mouth open. "Are you . . . real?"

Joyce let out a nervous laugh. "I am. Go ahead, touch me." She held out her arm.

Tentatively, Loretta poked Joyce's arm. She let out her breath in one big *whoosh*. "What are you doing here?"

"Walk with me?" Joyce bit her lip and looked relieved when Loretta nodded.

Loretta followed her to a quiet area by the pond, where a canopy of green leaves shaded them from the evening sun.

"I got your letter, and the portrait," Joyce said. "It's beautiful, Loretta."

Hearing Joyce say her name after so long made Loretta shiver. But she couldn't shake her confusion. "You didn't reply."

Joyce's mouth turned down. "I know, and I'm sorry about that. I should have answered, but I needed to figure out a few things first. That's what these are for." She held out the bouquet. "An apology bouquet. At least, that's what Eleanor told me. Each flower means . . . something. I can't remember, but Eleanor can tell you."

Loretta took the flowers, her fingers brushing Joyce's. Even though she'd touched her twice now, she still couldn't believe Joyce was really there. "Thanks." The flowers were pretty, but they didn't banish the tight feeling that had bloomed in Loretta's chest. "So you came here to . . . give me an apology bouquet?"

"No." Joyce stepped closer to her. "I mean, yes, I came here to apologize. But I also want to ask you something."

Loretta's heart thudded against her ribs. Her breathing became shallow. What was happening?

CHAPTER THIRTY-FOUR

JOYCE

Joyce had been terrified to show up at the Sunflower Festival that evening. She'd left Loretta hanging for so long, it was cruel. But she really had needed to figure things out. Could she feasibly move to Canada? Would Tori be okay with her moving halfway around the world after her fathers' recent move? How could Joyce ask Loretta to be together again in a way that meant something?

Now here Joyce was, back in Juniper Creek, at the festival that had ultimately united Minnie and Eleanor, and she didn't know how to take Loretta's reaction. Loretta didn't seem disappointed, and she was clearly shocked. But was she happy to see Joyce? There was only one way to find out.

"I know you asked if you could visit me in Scotland," Joyce said. "And while I'd love that, there's something I'd love even more." She took a moment to compose herself. "How would you feel about me staying in Juniper Creek?"

For the second time that evening, Loretta's jaw dropped. "What?"

"How would you feel if I stayed here? With you?"

To Joyce's astonishment, Loretta started laughing. The

scenario wasn't exactly funny, and Joyce waited anxiously as Loretta struggled to get ahold of herself.

"Sorry," Loretta said. "I just . . . What about Tori? I thought you wanted to be near her."

Joyce nodded. "I did. I still do, but I've realized that Tori doesn't need me as much as I thought she did. She's doing fine. Better than fine—she's doing really well. And she's got Burt, and the skipper who replaced Will knows what she's doing. I love my family, but they all have their own things going on now. I'm ready to take my own path too."

Joyce's voice had quieted, and Loretta stepped closer to her.

"Tori and I talked. She told me I shouldn't let go of what you and I have . . . or had. Even if it wasn't what I expected or planned for. I hope we still have it." She paused and took a deep breath. "Do we?" She felt her eyes widen involuntarily, likely reflecting her hope and fear.

"You want to stay? With me?" Loretta looked like she couldn't quite believe it, so Joyce needed to make herself as clear as possible.

"Yes. Loretta Vogel, I want to stay here in Juniper Creek. With you."

"Even if everyone around here names things after flowers?"

That made Joyce smile. "Yes. I would live forever in a world named after flowers if I could be with you."

Loretta laughed again, happiness radiating from her smile and the wrinkles around her forest-green eyes. "Then yes," she said. "We do still have . . . whatever we have."

A laugh bubbled out of Joyce as well, and Loretta flung her arms around her. "I missed you so much," she whispered into Joyce's hair.

"I missed you too."

They hugged for longer than was publicly acceptable, but Joyce didn't care. When they finally pulled apart, Loretta asked, "Can I kiss you?"

"Please do."

Loretta pressed her lips to Joyce's, one hand holding the bouquet and the other on the small of Joyce's back. "I love you," she murmured against Joyce's lips.

Joyce smiled and kissed Loretta's cheek. "I love you too. And I should have told you that earlier."

"I can't believe you're here."

"I can barely believe it myself."

"At the Sunflower Festival!"

"I know!"

"How long have you been here?"

"I got in yesterday . . ."

They ended up buying a bucket of kettle corn and walking around the pond, popping pieces in their mouths as they caught up with each other. When they reached the park again, the sun had gone almost all the way down, but the festival was still in full swing.

They found Minnie, Eleanor, Dylan, Frankie, Evvie, and Matthias sitting at a table near the gazebo. Dylan was petting one of the two dogs by her feet, and Minnie blinked blearily as if she could barely keep her eyes open. But the rest of them grinned at Joyce and Loretta.

Loretta set the bouquet gently on the table then put her hands on her hips. "You all knew about this, didn't you?"

Evvie giggled. "We might have had a hand in it."

"It seems to have worked out," Eleanor said with a smug arch of one delicate eyebrow.

"Maybe," Loretta replied, her nose in the air. "Matthias, you knew too?"

Matthias had been the first one Joyce had contacted. Since he was so close to his sister, she'd wanted his opinion about her coming back to town.

He gave her a cheeky grin. "Yeah, yeah. I knew."

After a split second of pretending to be offended, Loretta caved and hugged everyone at the table, even Dylan, who seemed taken aback.

"Thank you," Loretta said. She returned to Joyce's side, twining her fingers through Joyce's.

"Yes, thank you," Joyce echoed. "I'm knackered, though. Do you mind if we go to the farm? I'd like to say hi to the goddesses."

Loretta's answering expression sent Joyce's heart soaring. "Of course. They've missed you too."

On the ride to the farm, sitting beside Loretta in her worn little car, Joyce leaned her head back and inhaled the faint scent of lavender. She was home.

EPILOGUE

LORETTA

6 WEEKS LATER

*L*oretta let out a satisfied sigh and stared at the most beautiful chandeliers she'd ever seen hanging from the barn ceiling. Beautiful not only in their composition, but also in the way she'd acquired them. That rain-soaked night at the B&B with Joyce had changed her life for the better.

Speaking of . . .

"Have you seen Joyce?" Loretta asked one of the workers carrying in chairs. They had to set up the tables in the barn for the reception, and all the chairs needed to go to the loft for the cere-mony. The worker shook their head.

Loretta frowned. She wanted Joyce to sign off on the table layout—it seemed squishier than it looked on the seating plan—but she couldn't find her anywhere.

After checking the farmhouse once again and noting the almost-finished succulent puzzle on the kitchen table, she exited through the back door and found Joyce crouched by the chicken enclosure, cooing at Athena.

"There you are," Loretta said. "I've been looking for you."

"Have you? Well, I'm right here."

"I can see that."

Joyce stood and opened her arms for a hug. "What did you need me for?" she asked, pressing a soft kiss on Loretta's neck.

"The tables don't seem quite right."

"Let's have a look, then."

They quickly sorted out the problem: the groom's mother had brought her own table for the cake, which was larger than the original, so they had to shift a few things around.

"There," Joyce said, scanning the barn. "That should work. It'll be a tight fit with all the chairs, but it'll do."

"Thanks. I couldn't do this without you, you know," Loretta said.

"You could. You just wouldn't do it as well."

Loretta scoffed and lightly pushed Joyce's shoulder, but she smiled.

"I can't believe we're on wedding number two already," Loretta said. It hadn't even been a year since she'd decided to start this journey, and somehow she'd already hosted one wedding and was on the brink of another to kick off the fall season.

"I can." Joyce wrapped an arm around Loretta's waist. "Before you know it, you'll have hosted more events than you can count."

Loretta laughed. "We'll see." She paused, looking at the chandeliers she and Joyce had picked up together. "As long as you help me with them all."

"Of course."

They stood together, bathed in the light of the chandeliers, enjoying the cool breeze drifting in from the open barn door on the warm September night.

Home in each other's arms.

WANT MORE JUNIPER CREEK?

Sign up for Brenna Bailey's newsletter so you'll never miss a new release! You'll also get a free, exclusive short story with your newsletter subscription.

Get your free short story now!
www.brennabailey.com/newsletter

AUTHOR'S NOTE

I hope you enjoyed Joyce and Loretta's love story!

No matter what you thought of *Forever in Flowers*, please help your fellow readers by leaving a review on social media and your favorite reading platforms and stores. Reviews are hugely important for getting books in the hands of the right readers. Cheers!

ACKNOWLEDGMENTS

I am a white settler on Turtle Island, and I wrote this book in Moh'kinsstis in the Treaty 7 region of Southern Alberta. This is the traditional territory of the Blackfoot Confederacy, the Tsuut'ina, the Stoney Nakoda Nations, and the Métis Nation of Region 3. Land acknowledgments need to be about more than words—they need to be about action as well. I encourage you to donate to organizations that support and empower Indigenous communities. I will donate twenty percent of my release-day sales to the <u>Native Women's Association of Canada (NWAC)</u>.

I'll try to keep my thanks short and sweet, but so many people have supported me in the writing of this book.

Mom, Dad, Keegan, Tanya, Ron, Chris, Dustin, and Rachele, thank you for being the best family. Phoebe and Steph, I might only see you once a month, but it means a lot to me that we make an effort to be in each other's lives.

Orin, you keep me going every day. You are my number one story consultant and my life partner, and you remind me how important it is to play. January, you are the best cuddle buddy and fur baby on the entire planet.

Trisha Jenn Loehr, thank you for your feedback and encouragement! You have such a wonderful heart.

Molly Rookwood, your feedback on *Wishing on Winter* was instrumental in helping me write this book, and I am grateful for your guidance on writing authentic Jewish characters.

Jacquelynn Lyon and Todd Aasen, once again you helped improve this story and emboldened me during revisions.

Jessica Renwick, my wonderful editor, every time I work with you, I become a better writer and a better editor. Your edits and your friendship are invaluable.

Talena Winters and Jennifer E. Lindsay, thank you for providing a safe and empowering space to talk all things writing and editing. And Talena, thank you once again for writing my blurb!

Lucy from Cover Ever After, working on this entire series with you has been a dream. The cover for *Forever in Flowers* ties everything together beautifully.

And to each and every reader—I write for you. I hope this book brings you as much joy as you bring me.

ALSO BY BRENNA BAILEY

Juniper Creek Golden Years Series
"I Want to Hold Your Hand" (short story)
A Tale of Two Florists
Of Love and Libraries
Wishing on Winter

Image Description: Photo of Brenna smiling at the camera. She is a white woman with curly blond hair and glasses, and she's wearing a blue shirt. End of description.

Brenna Bailey writes queer contemporary romance and owns an editing business called Bookmarten Editorial. If her nose isn't buried in a book, you can probably find her out in the woods somewhere admiring plants or attempting to identify birds. She is a starry-eyed traveler and a home baker, and she lives in Calgary, Alberta, with her game-loving spouse and their cuddly fur-baby.

instagram.com/brennabaileybooks

www.ingramcontent.com/pod-product-compliance
Lightning Source LLC
Chambersburg PA
CBHW061204210726
48294CB00006B/1748